Tears of the *Innocent*

Ugomma Ngozi

Tears of the Innocent
Copyright © 2024 by Ugomma Ngozi

All rights reserved. No part of this publication may be reproduced,
distributed, or transmitted in any form or by any means, including
photocopying, recording, or other electronic or mechanical
methods, without the prior written permission of the author, except
in the case of brief quotations embodied in critical reviews and
certain other non-commercial uses permitted by copyright law.

Library of Congress Control Number: 2024923668

ISBN
978-1-964488-35-6 (Paperback)
978-1-964488-36-3 (eBook)
978-1-964488-34-9 (Hardcover)

Written for You

Table of Contents

Acknowledgment

The author gratefully acknowledges the Living God, Jesus Christ, my savior, for making the existence of this book possible and for being forever self-existent in my life. "By my God I can leap over a wall." The Word of God said in Zechariah 4:6, "It's not by might nor by power but by my Spirit." While I was going through many difficulties in life, God turned them into miracles by changing my thoughts around. Instead of crying my head off while my heart was being torn apart, God taught me that all things were possible.

When I was too tired to stand up through these tribulations, God inspired me by giving me the strength I needed to rise up again. When I couldn't figure things out by myself, God directed my steps. When I believed I couldn't do it anymore, God reminded me that with his powers bestowed upon me, I could do all things. When I knew in my mind that I could no longer go on, God reminded me that his grace was sufficient for me. When I was always worried and frustrated, God grabbed away all my sorrows and worries and carried them. When I felt all alone, God reminded me that he would never leave me nor forsake me. When I believed that I could no longer manage, God told me that he would supply all my need. When I felt low and rejected, God turned this rejected stone now into this chief cornerstone. I could go on and on, but it would never be enough. All I can say now is I give God the glory for the gift and courage he bestowed upon me into writing this book.

The author acknowledges Mr. and Mrs. Samuel Onyechere Ibezim. You have done your job, and you have done it well. To Mr. Samuel Onyechere Ibezim, thank you for being my best friend when no one else was. Thank you for giving me a memorable childhood like no one else could. May God bless you beyond imagination for being a great, loving, caring, philanthropic grandfather to me (rest in peace).

To Mrs. Stella Iheakara Ibezim, thank you for teaching me love, values, respect, honor, integrity, and God. Thank you for waking up at 5:30 a.m. every morning to get me ready for kindergarten school bus (nursery school bus). Thank you for making sure I never had to eat the hospital food when I had typhoid fever and was hospitalized. Thank you for seeing my pain and wiping away my tears when no one else could. Thank you for giving me a memorable childhood like no one else. May God bless you beyond words and beyond anyone's imagination for being a great, loving, caring, philanthropic, etc., grandmother to me (rest in peace).

Thank you, Ogechika Ukaegbu, Chidiebere Ukaegbu, my wonderful sister and brother for being my best friends, for being there for laughter when needed, and for playing your intended roles in my life. May the Almighty keep you both straight and strong in Jesus's name.

Finally, the author acknowledges her editors, all those who helped in making sure that the publication and the distribution of this book are possible; and of course, the author gratefully acknowledges the readers.

WRITTEN FOR YOU

The Bible quotations in this book are from the King James Version.

Unfortunately, we are living in the last days, also known as the days of famine or the days of tribulations and afflictions. These are the days when parents no longer see or think of the importance of their children's future. We are living in the days when children no longer see the significance of their parents. We are living in the days when our friends and families have more important things to do than to love and care for us. Most people consider these days to be the worst days of their lives. As for me, I consider it to be the best rather than the worst days of our lives. The Bible says in Psalm 27:10, "When my father and my mother forsake me, then the Lord will care for me." This is the best days of our lives because in God, we have better parents, a better friend, and a trustworthy companion.

This is a story of a girl's life, which started tragically and went downhill from there. Although as a little girl, she was forced to go to church by her families like most families today do with their children. After all the tribulations and pains she went through and how things turned out for her, she decided to give her life to the one she believed could carry her through it all. She gave her life to *Jesus Christ*.

The purpose of this book is to encourage, aspire, inspire, and also help most—if not all—of our children, preteens, young adults, and parents in making the right decisions no matter the tribulations you should be passing through.

To see what giving your life to God can really do for you, this book tells you the tragedies this young girl passed through. Read the second part of this book titled *The Joy of Hannah* (forthcoming), and from this you would see how the many ways on how passing through the difficulties of life while in the hands of God can deliver you.

CHAPTER ONE

UNEXPECTED BEGINNING

This is the story of Hannah and how her life turned from a rejected stone as a child to a chief cornerstone as a woman through the grace and the love of her God and savior, Jesus Christ. The story that started off tragically ended up making her the better and stronger person she is today. Through the pains and suffering she went through, she received the courage, strength, faith, wisdom, knowledge, patience, hope, understanding, miracle, signs, and wonders she needed to make it through life.

The Bible says in Psalm 30:3, "For his anger endures but for a moment; in his favor is life: weeping may endure for a night, but joy comes in the morning." Unlike most people that learn about God through family members, friends, or just the outsiders, although Hannah was forced to go to church every Sundays as a little girl, she did not learn about God through church, families, friends, or even the outsiders; rather she learned about God through God himself.

Born in 1980 in United Kingdom, Hannah was raised in Nigeria by her grandparents, while her parents were from Nigeria but lived in United Kingdom. This tragic life of Hannah started soon after 10 of December 1980. In the earlier years before that, her mother, Sandra, met and befriended an amazing and respected lawyer, Mr. Jude, and his family, Mrs. Lucy from Ghana and their daughters, Love and Brenda. In 1979, the lawyer's spouse—while in Ghana for a visit—died in a car accident.

The two beautiful girls were now left behind with their father at ages one and three years old, without a mother. Their father, being a lawyer, was always very busy in both his career and his family, and this was too much for him to handle alone. During this period, Hannah's mother, Ms. Sandra, heard the news of the death of her good friend and, out of sympathy, volunteered to move in to help the lawyer and the two children both emotionally and physically.

She moved in, and in less than three months after moving in, she got pregnant; and the lawyer, not wanting to carry the shame of having an unplanned child with Sandra, decided to marry her. On December 10, 1980, Hannah was born in London.

During the pregnancy, the horror began in the sense that Hannah's mother changed and took a turn for the worse. Growing up, Hannah's mother, Sandra, was the first of her mother's seven children. With this being the case, she was so spoiled by her parents that she got anything that she wanted, including getting her parents to sell a part of their land back in Nigeria in order to send her to the United Kingdom. Although Hannah's mother was very intelligent, her way of living when it came to having things her way was about to ruin both her life and the lives of her new family.

Soon after the marriage, she found out that both she and the lawyer had different plans about their future. She was a very hardworking woman who loved her independence and would rather work as opposed to staying at home and caring for the children, while the lawyer was in need of a spouse who would stay home and care for his children. This became the biggest hindrance in their marriage. She became very stubborn and would not listen to reasons, and the lawyer became highly frustrated because his job took up much of his time and he needed some help with his children. At this time, Mrs. Sandra's mother, Mrs. Grace, and her two sisters came from Nigeria to help her.

The lawyer became the type of person known as a silent killer in the sense that he became highly abusive to Hannah's mother privately. As he constantly abused her, the lawyer's wrongs overshadowed Mrs. Sandra's wrongs because she took out that pain on everyone else in the family, including her own daughter, Hannah.

In many occasions, Mrs. Grace, Sandra's sisters, and the children—Love, Brenda, and Hannah—became the strong victims of this situation. Sandra took out her emotional pain and anger on everyone in the house, and the lawyer took out his pain and anger on Sandra privately. It got so bad to the point that at three months old, Hannah stopped breastfeeding from Sandra and Sandra started taking out her angers and pains even on her only daughter, Hannah. Being an infant in need of attention, Hannah developed a habit of how to keep herself busy by sitting and hitting her back on the wall. The same children that Mrs. Sandra was supposed to care for, she abused to the point of almost having them thrown out of the house.

Mrs. Sandra became so uncooperative to the lawyer and everyone in the family to the point that the lawyer almost lost his license as a lawyer, and almost 95 percent of the Nigerians who were living in the UK knew all about this family. Due to the physical and emotional abuse Mrs. Sandra's mother was receiving, Mrs. Grace decided to go back to Nigeria. Though things were bad with these couples, the lawyer found the time for his three special girls. He tried to always make the time to play and spend with his three children.

The couple, after a while, agreed that it was not a good decision after all getting married and therefore agreed to get divorce. When they went to the court for a divorce, the judge saw the truth and the evidence that the lawyer was not after all the innocent man he claimed to be and therefore awarded Sandra the custody of their child, Hannah, and Sandra took Hannah back to Nigeria.

From this chapter we get to learn more of what great change real love can bring in people's life and what wicked separation the spirit of pride can do to people. After all, it is the spirit of pride that separated God from the Devil. We get to learn that true love that comes with sacrifice would also turn things around.

It is, after all, the love that our Heavenly Father has for his children that made him pull himself so low to the point of sacrificing himself for us, and from his death, his children got the second chance we have today.

If Mr. Jude, the lawyer, truly loved Mrs. Sandra, he would have had faith and patience instead of abusing his spouse for her wrongdoing. Being the man of the house makes him also the teacher and the leader of his household. All he needed to do was teach his spouse about meekness from living the life of humility, and perhaps from watching Mr. Jude, Mrs. Sandra would have learned the right way of living, which would have made a very big difference.

With this chapter we should see that true love destroys the spirit of pride and resurrects the spirit of meekness, faith, patience, and many more that can only heal instead of breaking the heart.

Chapter Two

Tears of the Innocent

Before Sandra married her spouse, Mr. Jude, she was studying to get her doctorate degree, but with the marriage and everything in between, she stopped. With the marriage being over, Sandra called her school to check if the offer given to her was still available. When she was told that it was still available, she quickly took it and left Hannah with her grandparents back in their town in Lagos.

Before this period, Mrs. Sandra took Hannah with her for a while as she looked for a job in Abuja in Nigeria. As young as Hannah was, she could still remember being left alone in a small room while her mother goes out in search for a job. Normally, Mrs. Sandra would leave Hannah in that one bedroom with one of Sandra's male friends, Joseph, and leave for the day. Joseph would leave a bottle of Coca-Cola for Hannah and would leave her alone until when her mother comes back, which may not be the same day. Hannah would sit there by the wall and cry until she sleeps. When she wakes up, she would resume sitting, hitting her back at the wall, and this became Hannah's daily routine. There were some days that she would go on without eating or seeing her mother, although Joseph would normally come every day and give her a bottle of Coca-Cola to drink.

This is where you get to learn that God indeed was with this little girl because most children would not survive such treatment and still make it both mentally and physically.

One day, what used to be a friendly visit from Joseph became a nightmare when Joseph began to molest her in many ways. Though he did not succeed in tearing Hannah apart, Hannah however, being a little girl, became very scared that she would just sit there by the wall, shivering each time she sees him and hitting her back on the wall. It's very sad to say that this child was experiencing the molestation every one in three children today goes through. Hannah would always wish her mother would just come and be with her. Joseph would always molest Hannah each time he came, and due to the physical pain she would be going through, she would start screaming and crying. Whenever Hannah's mother came back, she would go and bring the same guy before coming in the room as she chats and laughs with him. Mrs. Sandra would thank Joseph for taking care of Hannah, not knowing of course or even caring what her little daughter went through during the period while she was gone.

After molesting Hannah for a while in his many ways, Joseph went deeper by trying now to rape this little girl. Hannah one day cried in a loud voice for her mother to pay attention and to listen to her as she complains to her mother of what Joseph was doing to her, but Mrs. Sandra paid little to no attention to her daughter. As a three-year-old little girl not knowing any better, Hannah would just sit there and hit her back at the wall, assuming maybe her mother has abandoned her because she was either ugly or perhaps, she was a bad little girl unworthy of her mother's love, or maybe her mother just really hated her.

It's very sad to say, but this is precisely what many children go through, especially in these days that lead children, preteens, teenagers, young adults, or even older adults into the wrong path of life just to make it through. However, though Hannah had no mother or father to look after her, as the Word of the Lord said on Romans 9:15, "I will have mercy on whom I have mercy, and I will have compassion on whom I have compassion." God had mercy on her and, therefore, kept her safe and in great health. At the age of four, Hannah was taken by Mrs. Sandra to her grandparents' house, where she was finally given the love, she really needed, hoped, wished, and cried for.

From this chapter, we get to learn that no matter what we go through in life, God could never give us more than we can handle, and he is always there for us when we need him. God would be there to play that role of a friend, a brother, a sister, a mother, and a father to one who has none. He is the father to the fatherless and the mother to the motherless, and with him, we would always make it no matter what tribulations we pass through in life.

CHAPTER THREE

ALMOST PERFECT!
(DOES IT REALLY COUNT?)

Around the age of four years old, Hannah was taken by Ms. Sandra to her grandparents, who raised the angel in their town. Ms. Sandra left Hannah with them, and Hannah never saw her mother again until she was around the age of seven years when her grandfather passed away.

Until Hannah started living with her grandparents, she never knew that life could ever be so sweet. Her grandfather, Mr. Nnamdi, became her best friend. Everywhere he went, he took her with him, and Hannah was nicknamed Daddy's Little Eagle. With him around, no one else mattered and no one else existed. He was Hannah's hero and her greatest friend sent from above. Hannah was never wrong in his eyes. Even when she was wrong, he would correct her without yelling or screaming. Hannah always listened and tried not to do whatever he didn't want her to do and did whatever he wanted her to do. He spoilt her so much that no one could send Hannah on any type of house message around him. Hannah always did the right thing just to make him happy. These days became Hannah's happy and terror-free days.

Along with Hannah, the grandparents were also raising five other children in their house, three granddaughters and two of Hannah's uncles, James and Nnamdi II, who was the first son of the household. And of them all, Hannah was the last. The first granddaughter was Brittany, and she was eight years older than Hannah. The second was Charity and was almost two years older than Hannah. Hannah was the only one that was born in the UK and was very light skinned at the time.

For those three years of being away from her mother, Hannah forgot all about the fear, pain, and constant sorrows she went through during the period she lived with her mother due to the joy she experienced while living with her grandparents. She was in her new place, but of course, all that was about to change because Ms. Sandra had to come back during her father's burial and so had the horrific memories already implanted in Hannah's heart. Just as Hannah saw her mother's face again, all those painful memories started coming back to her. It was as if Hannah was reliving the horror all over. Her mother came back into her life and saw the love and the trust Hannah had for her grandmother and, moreover, the happiness in the eyes of her daughter and, of course, did her very best to destroy that happiness.

Ms. Sandra wanted to take away the love and trust Hannah had for her grandmother by advising her to steal from her grandmother and to displease her. However, thankfully, though Hannah was a little girl, her grandparents taught her right from wrong, and she could differentiate from real love and fake love. And Hannah knew her grandmother loved her, but her mother only pretended to love her. At times, Hannah would wonder if her mother had bipolar disorder due to her change in mood toward her.

Growing up there in Nigeria, they normally did not celebrate occasions such as birthdays and Christmas the way it was celebrated in the cities or overseas by buying presents for your friends and families.

Instead, they celebrated it by boiling a big pot of rice, which is a big thing at times, and using many goat meat or fish to make a big pot of stew. However, Hannah's case was different. Being that her mother was always traveling around, she would send Hannah presents such as clothes, shoes, etc., which would of course make Hannah's friends and cousins jealous of her, though those materialistic things never really mattered much to her compared to the love she was receiving from her families and her friends.

On one occasion, Ms. Sandra asked Hannah for what she called a favor, which was stealing money from her grandmother and bringing it to her. Hannah, being smarter than her mother though, did just as she said, but instead of stealing from her grandmother, she stole from Ms. Sandra. Ms. Sandra was very unhappy as she was looking for her money. Hannah said nothing for a while until later that day, Hannah went and gave her the money and said to her, "This is what you wanted me to do to a woman who has fed, clothed, sheltered, and loved me when you couldn't." She knew then that Hannah would never love her the way she loved her grandmother and immediately revealed the truth about Hannah's biological father to Hannah, knowing how destructive it would be, at that age, to her.

Ms. Sandra came to Hannah about her biological father, but of course, not trusting the words of her mother, Hannah asked her grandmother; and her grandmother confirmed it and told Hannah that her father loves her and would always love her. Hannah's grandmother then started telling Hannah about her two big sisters and how they would chase, play, and run around when she was still in the United Kingdom in her father's house, calling Hannah their Little Jaja. With this in Hannah's mind, she wanted to know more about her biological father and her big sisters. So she began to track him down. First, she wrote a letter and gave it to one of her aunts that came from United Kingdom for her grandfather's burial to give to her father. Every time Hannah knew of someone that was going to the United Kingdom that knew her father, she would write a letter for him, but through it all, Hannah never received a response from her father.

Shortly after Mr. Nnamdi's death, Hannah became ill with typhoid fever, during which time Ms. Sandra was in the city working. Hannah's body's complexion changed and became very white. Her grandmother did not have much money, and her mother was not around to provide the money needed. Back in that country, unlike most developed countries, the hospital would want their payment before providing any treatment to their patients. Her grandmother, being more concerned with Hannah's health, borrowed the money needed for the treatments. While in the hospital, Hannah consumed seven pipes of drips and three pipes of blood. At this time, while in the hospital, Hannah learned what real love and compassion was about when her grandmother and her cousin Charity made sure she never ate the hospital food. Every morning when she wakes up before the hospital would bring their food, her grandmother or her cousin or both would be by her bedside with breakfast. The same was the case in the afternoon and in the evening. They would always go home, cook food, and bring it for her.

Hannah's grandmother, Mrs. Grace, was always there with her. Her never-ending love, tenderness, and care were the only medicine Hannah needed to get better. If Hannah was not sure before of her cousin Charity and her grandmother's love for her, this was definitely a concrete assurance.

Ms. Sandra came for a home visit sometime that month, and Mrs. Grace told her about the illness and how much it cost. But instead of Ms. Sandra being grateful for the good deeds toward Hannah, she started asking for money from Mrs. Grace. Although Mrs. Grace had a little store where she sold school supplies, they had just barely enough to eat. However, Mrs. Grace still managed to give Hannah's mother sixty thousand naira. After receiving the money, Ms. Sandra thought the money was too little and tore the money apart and started screaming at her mother. The neighbors that witnessed it or heard the yelling came and started screaming at Ms. Sandra. They all expressed their feelings, explaining to her that she was supposed to be the one giving her mother money as opposed to taking money from her own mother. After they yelled and screamed at Ms. Sandra, she said nothing and left the house with shame.

Not too long after leaving the hospital, maybe after five months, did the second phase of Hannah's horror begin. Since her grandfather was dead and could no longer watch over her, her uncles saw an open space and did not hesitate to take it. Before Hannah's grandfather passed away, her grandmother had always cared for her and showered her with love; but with her grandfather around, Hannah did not pay much attention to the grandmother. Hannah's grandfather passed away, and immediately, Mrs. Grace took his place. But of course, for an old woman, the amount of protection she could give was not the same as the grandfather.

Hannah's uncles became very fond of Hannah, especially after her grandparent's death, and Hannah always thought it was because she was the last baby of the house. They nicknamed her Eagle's Baby. Hannah's younger uncle was always on the road, but her Uncle Nnamdi II rarely traveled and not too long after their father's death did he start taking Hannah around wherever he went. To Hannah at the time, he did this because he loved her and wanted to fill that void in Hannah's heart. Little did she know that he had ulterior motives, and that motive was not going to benefit Hannah; instead, it would add more confusion to her already crashed emotional state.

One day, when Hannah was a little over seven years old, Hannah's grandmother left to visit one of her friends. Her eldest cousin left with her friend, and Hannah was in the living room hitting her head on the wall as she normally did whenever she was alone. Charity was in the backyard relaxing. Her Uncle Nnamdi called Hannah's cousin and sent her to go buy something for him, and as she left, he called Hannah to his room and began to touch her in a sinful manner. At first, Hannah thought about her mother's friend and the way he used to touch her but then assumed that since this was her uncle, he would not hurt her in that manner. He started to undress Hannah, and she got scared that she started shivering but did nothing else. He then started again to molest her in the same way her mother's friend molested her, and he threatened to whip Hannah if she would tell anybody what happened. And due to that threat, Hannah was so afraid and kept it to herself. This went on for years, but out of fear, she handled it and cried only in private where no one would see her. She told no one about it for years.

Each time he had the opportunity to get her to himself, he would take it, and each time, he would molest her until he started raping her and she started bleeding and crying. This happened almost every day. When everybody is in bed, he would wake her up and ask her to escort him somewhere. Although Hannah did not want to go, out of the intimidation and fear, she would get up and go with him. This became his daily routine upon her, and one day, he started asking Hannah if her period had started. Each time, she would answer no without any clue as to why he asked.

Hannah's Uncle James was always traveling and did not do to Hannah what his brother was doing to her. For a while, Hannah believed her Uncle James was the good uncle, but little did she know that the role of an uncle he played in her life was only for a little while. One day, he came back from one of his journeys and called Hannah in his room to help him unpack. As Hannah was helping him, he stopped and started staring at her. Hannah stopped as she noticed him looking at her and asked him why he was staring at her. He said to her because she was growing up and was so beautiful, and Hannah started laughing and replied, "Thank you, Uncle." Then he started touching her the same way his brother was touching her, and from experiences Hannah has received, she stopped laughing and started shivering and crying in a very low voice. He looked at her and then stopped and asked her to go and clean her tears. The next time, he waited till Hannah's grandmother left the house and his brother went out with his friend, and her eldest cousin was never in the house because she always went out with her friend. Then he called her other cousin Charity and asked her to go and buy something for him. He then called Hannah and started molesting her as usual, the same way her other uncle molested her.

This became the process and the abuse Hannah received from her own uncles until she was around twelve years old. At this point, of course, you would think the life of this little girl was ending, considering all the abuse she received not just from strangers but also from her own family members. But of course, out of the mercies and the love of God upon her, she survived it all. As the Word of God said in 1 Thessalonians 5:18, "In everything give thanks: for this is the 'will' of God in Christ Jesus concerning you." Although no one could see and know what was happening to Hannah, God knew and saw all things. And with him by you, you will pass through all the tribulations and overcome all, understanding that God will never give you more than you can handle.

As this process continued, one day, her Uncle James sent Charity out as usual but did not finish with Hannah on time before Charity came back. And as Charity saw Hannah crying in a low voice as she was walking out of his room, she asked Hannah what happened; but out of fear, she tried to lie. But Charity could see it in her eyes that something was troubling Hannah and therefore took her to the backyard and persuaded her to tell her what happened. So Hannah told her, and immediately, she started crying for Hannah and forced her to tell their grandmother what was going on.

The next day, Hannah summoned the courage to tell her grandmother what had been going on, but of course, for an old woman, all she could do was cry with her and after which yelled at her two only sons for having done what they had been doing. Through this, the family finally found out the incident that was occurring and did their very best to stop it.

As I said before, the Word of God in 1 Thessalonians 5:18, "In everything give thanks: for this is the 'will' of God in Christ Jesus concerning you." Although staying in her grandparents' house caused her pains from her uncles, however, staying here was also one of the best things that could have ever happened to her in the sense that the greatest experiences that Hannah had in her life were not just with her grandparent, but also with the lifelong friends she ended up with from this house.

As a little girl, Hannah, I am sure, could never be convinced that there were better friends in the world than the ones she had growing up. One of her best friends was Kenneth, and he was her age and was like a brother to her. They did everything together, including going to the stream to get water.

Her other best friend was Princess, and she was two years younger than her, and they played like they were one. They all did almost everything together, along with her other friends Nkechi, Chineye, Chidinma, Nnamdi, and Uchenna, who helped brighten up her childhood.

Although Hannah's uncles almost destroyed what was left of Hannah, both physical and emotional, she however would be forever grateful that there were still many others there who helped in teaching her manners and morals. They really helped a lot in disciplining, teaching, and correcting her whenever she needed training as a growing young teenager to-be.

Living with her grandparents was one of the best things that could have ever happened to her, not because she was spoiled by both her grandparents or because of the abuses she received from her uncles while living there, but because she ended up with the best friends anyone could ever have. She was never alone anymore and, most importantly, learned morals, honor, love, trust, care, respect, and much more. The very thing we lack today in most countries and societies, especially in developed countries, Hannah learned all in this town with the best families and friends she would love and cherish for the rest of her life.

From this chapter we get to learn that even in the worst tribulations and difficulties, God always provides for us other ways to keep us moving higher, and God is always there with his soldiers to clean our pools of tears and open other doors that would help us forget the sorrow and only feel the joy and happiness surrounding us. We also learn, as the Word of God says in 1 Corinthians 10:13, "There hath no temptation taken you but such as is common to man; but God is faithful, who will not suffer you to be tempted above that ye are able, but will with the temptation also make a way to escape, that ye may be able to bear it."

Although sad to say, but these talks of rape and molestations are what many go through these days, especially children, preteens, teenagers, and young adults. This book is written in order to encourage you to have faith in God and believe that you are being tempted because the enemy is trying to destroy your destiny written by God. With the resurrection powers bestowed upon us, we are capable of winning every battle against the enemy. All it takes is to have that strong faith and patience in God, knowing that all things are possible if we just believe.

From this chapter we also learn that though we today would be going through more tribulations than we believe we can handle, God knows just how to turn our sorrows, agonies, pains, difficulties, and tribulations into miracles just as he changed Hannah's sorrows into miracles with her new great, wonderful, and endless friends and also the family members that only loved her beyond spoken words, such as her grandparents and her best cousin Charity. All it takes to win is to call and wait on God. Wait on him as you call him, knowing that he sees you and he is always there and ready to fight for you. All it takes it to have faith and to call on him.

CHAPTER FOUR

HER EARLY SCHOOL DAYS

Not shortly after her release from the hospitals, Hannah started her nursery school (kindergarten). Hannah's mother put her in a private nursery school close to her grandparent's house. The fact that her mother, of all the kindergartens, chose to enroll her in an expensive private school made Hannah believe that her mother loves and wants the best for her, but then again, at times her mother ignored Hannah when Hannah needed her most.

Every morning, Hannah's grandmother would wake up at around 5:30 a.m., or maybe 5:40 a.m., to get Angel ready for school because the school bus comes to the house to pick her up at around 6:30 a.m. Every morning, when Mrs. Grace would get her ready for school, Hannah would wait until the school bus comes to the house then would start crying. She would cry continuously for her grandmother to give her one of the candies that Mrs. Grace, her grandmother, sells, and Mrs. Grace eventually would have no choice but to give Hannah the candy because she couldn't stand watching Hannah cry. And whenever

Hannah came back from school, her grandmother would prepare lunch for her; and after eating, Hannah would go out to play with her friends. As time went on, the sorrows Hannah had in her heart concerning her grandfather's death faded away because her grandmother was filling up that hole in her heart.

Around this time, Hannah was also mature enough to help out with the house chores. She started going to the farm with her cousins and her grandmother and farming with them as well as going to the stream to fetch water with her cousins and friends. The second best time of her life started because now she started hanging out with these children that would end up becoming her best friends and make her childhood a blessing. Most of Hannah's friends were around her age group, and they all did everything together. Life was sweet at this point because even though her uncles continued their evil ways toward her, Hannah had friends and her grandmother that healed all the physical and emotional pains by bestowing upon her those emotional blessing and unforgettable joyful memories.

Hannah and her cousins started going to the farm together, which was in the rainy seasons. After their grandmother taught them how to crop, they took over—especially now that Mrs. Grace was getting older. Hannah and her cousins would normally eat in the morning and then go off to the farm to crop. They would farm, chat, and laugh among each other until around the evening time. By that time, their grandmother would cook food and bring it for them. After which they would then leave for the day. This was especially fun because she and her cousins would be having fun while cropping to the point that they would do so much work without even knowing it.

One year later, Hannah was done with kindergarten and was now off to elementary school, and around this time, Hannah's uncles started forcing themselves on her. Her mother came back from one of her travels, and Hannah told her mother what her uncles were doing to her; but of course, the mother did not care or pay attention to the report and therefore barely responded to Hannah. Traveling back to the city, Ms. Sandra took Hannah with her as it was now time for Hannah to go to primary school (middle school). Being a little girl that was not used to traveling, Hannah was very excited and ready to get away from her uncles, although she would miss her dear friends. It was as if Hannah should know by now that her emotional state was taking a turn for the worse. It was like going from a burning building to boiling-hot water. It felt as though the older she got, the more confused she was destined to become.

Through it all, Hannah gave her mother credit for one thing, and that was for putting her in the best private schools. As for Hannah's elementary school, her mother put her in one of the best elementary schools in the world. Although Hannah was born in a better-developed and well-educated country, she grew up in an underdeveloped environment and therefore did not learn correct English. Coming to this school gave her that opportunity to learn the correct way to speak proper English. While attending this school, Hannah moved around a lot because Ms. Sandra did not have a permanent place for her to stay. She lived with different friends of her mother.

One of the friends she lived with was her mother's divorced male friend who had three boys, and they lived in a small apartment. Hannah was the youngest of all of them and the only girl, excluding their house help, who was a grown woman. Their father had a private ride for his children to get to school while Ms. Sandra gave Hannah some money to take a taxi as a way of getting to school, being that the school was about eight to ten miles away from the house. Being that Hannah did not have any other way of getting money, she would walk sometimes to school in order to save the money for junk food while in school. Whenever Hannah's mother comes to visit, these boys would report Hannah to Ms. Sandra that they saw her walking home from school, and Ms. Sandra would yell at her. Hannah lived with this family for about two years, and while living with them, they believed Hannah's mother to be an amazing woman because she always gave Hannah money for transportation and also visited them. Hannah started telling these boys about the bad things her mother had done to both her and her family (namely her grandmother). She told them that she hated her mother for everything that she put her through, and these boys threatened to tell Hannah's mother all that Hannah said about her. But of course, as a child, Hannah was afraid of what her mother would do, especially in public, if she should hear the news and therefore promised to do whatever these boys wanted to stop them from telling on her. On many occasions, the boys would force Hannah to give them some of the money her mother gave her, and Hannah would have no choice but to give. After two years plus, she was about eleven plus years and was done for the semester. After a few months, her mother came and took her out of her friend's house for a new level of life.

From this chapter again we get to learn that no matter what we go through in life, God is really the one carrying our burdens. God would always open another door to move your pain, your sorrows, your agonies into happiness, peace, and joy and great memories to move you through. Though Hannah did not have a simple and an easy life to live, but as the Word of God said in Psalm 46:1, "God is our refuge and strength, a very present help in trouble." Though life was difficult for Hannah, God took over that burden, and she still survived it all and made it through even with the tribulations and pain she passed through.

CHAPTER FIVE

TRIBULATIONS UPON TRIBULATIONS

Now school was done, and it was time for Hannah to go back home to her amazing friends and tender-loving grandmother but at the same time to her abusive, insensitive uncles.

Of course, some part of her would be happy to go home to a place she would never be alone, being with her grandmother and her loving friends, but at the same time, Hannah was so afraid of going back home knowing what awaits her when it came to her uncles and their physical abuses toward her.

Coming back home was supposed to be an exciting event, but due to an incident that occurred while she was away that she was informed of, Hannah's whole excitement disappeared. She arrived to the house to find numerous neighbors standing by their house with a sad look on their face and her grandmother nowhere to be found. Hannah started asking about her grandmother, only to find out that she was put in prison. Hannah saw one of her aunt yelling and screaming at her mother and became even more confused. The law enforcement policy where they lived was very different from the law enforcement in most developed and underdeveloped countries. Their law enforcement runs with the motto of Money Equals Power. With Hannah's mother, Ms. Sandra, being a PhD holder practically gave her the right to imprison everyone in her family without cause so long as she was able to bribe the police with money. Hannah came home to find out that her grandmother was imprisoned by her mother. From the information, Hannah started fighting and arguing with her mother and went to the police station and asked them to release her grandmother immediately but having no money for the police did not accomplish anything doing so. Although Mrs. Grace was not there for more than twenty-four hours, she was an elderly woman at the time and needed much care, and when Hannah heard the news, she became so furious with her mother to the point that she wanted Ms. Sandra to leave the house. Ms. Sandra insisted on staying, and Hannah, out of anger, threw down all of Ms. Sandra's wet washed clothes outside in the sand and filled up her room with buckets of water, damaging several of her valuables, while her mother, out of fear of what else Hannah would do, just sat in her room and said nothing.

Although Hannah was the youngest in her grandfather's house, she was also the only one that could deal with her mother on her level. In other words, she was the only person that could be as wicked to her mother as she was to everyone else. Although Hannah was very strong physically due to hard labor and experiences in life, she was not a fighter but was rather an angry person that could easily throw anything at anyone in quarrel, especially heavy stones. Ms. Sandra, being well aware what her daughter was capable of doing in anger, left Hannah's presence immediately, saying and doing nothing. Ms. Sandra, remembering that Hannah's father, Mr. Jude, was physical to her in his anger, believed that Hannah did not only look like her father but also acted like him as well when it comes to her reactions when she is unhappy.

Hannah's uncles then went to the police station and brought their mother out of prison. The love Hannah had for her grandmother was so strong that Ms. Sandra had no chance at all. Of course, the minute Ms.

Sandra left the house the happiness and joy came back to their home. Ms. Grace, being such a strong woman, came back from the prison and immediately started cooking and feeding everybody and especially made a special welcome present dinner for Hannah. Mrs. Grace was like an angel sent from above to Hannah in the sense that whenever Mrs. Gracc was around, Hannah remembers nothing else about the tribulations and difficulties that may have happened to her in the past.

Not long after the holiday was up, Hannah went back to school. In the year 1990, Hannah came back from her next school holiday to receive what she believed to be one of her sad news as a little girl, which was the fact that her older cousins, who she also knew to be her big sisters, would be traveling to London in United Kingdom where their parents currently lived. Saying good-bye, of course, would not be easy, but this, of course, Hannah had to endure. She felt lonely and lost not just because of having to stay there with her abusive, insensitive uncles but also having no one to console her but her grandmother. Hannah's cousins left her and went to London, and Hannah was now all alone in the house whenever she came back from school holidays.

Luckily for Hannah she did not have to stay long before she went off for high school. Though Ms. Sandra didn't know much when it comes to being a tender, loving mother, she would be given good credit for always making sure Hannah received the best educational system, and in so doing Hannah yet again ended up in a private and a burdensome high school.

Although leaving her grandmother's house was for a good purpose, which is to continue her education, it was however very painful for Hannah to leave, though she would still be coming back home every holidays. Having felt the way Hannah felt about her mother, she could not see and appreciate anything good her mother did for her. Normally in boarding school they have what are called visiting days, and these are when your parents or guardian would be expected to come and bring some provisions—which are snacks for their children, to carry them through until the next visiting days. Hannah's school was so far from her grandparents' house and Hannah's grandmother, being now elderly, could not visit her on visiting days; so on every visitation days, Hannah would just sit there and watch other girls happy with their parents and families while she cries, having no family member there for her. Though Hannah's friends would share whatever food and provisions they received from their parents and/or guardian with her, but of course, one would know receiving from your own families would be different and more special.

From coming to this school, Ms. Sandra introduced Hannah to one of Hannah cousin's, Nadia, who was around Angel's age. Nadia's parents were very rich and gave her everything she wanted. Every visiting day, she would bring Hannah some food and snacks. Hannah's mom has a way of convincing everyone else around her that she was the best mother on earth and managed to do just that. Even though she never came to see Hannah on any visiting days, she managed to convince everyone that she couldn't because she was too busy.

Nadia believed that Hannah's mother was a great mother. Hannah, not having anyone to talk to as a real friend, bottled so much of her pains in her mind and decided to turn to her new cousin, thinking her cousin would understand her, but instead Nadia made Hannah her enemy when Hannah told Nadia how evil her mother was to her. Nadia had already believed Ms. Sandra to be the best and therefore assumed Hannah was lying against her mother until the end of the school year when Hannah's mom didn't come to get Hannah.

It was the end of the school year, and everyone left, including Hannah's cousin, believing of course that Hannah's mom would come and pick Hannah. To Nadia's surprise two weeks later, everyone has left but Hannah. Nadia came back to the school to get something she forgot only to see her cousin there all alone, and so she signed Hannah out with her driver and took Hannah to their house. Ms. Sandra did not come to their house until after one and a half month later after the school closing date. From that day, Nadia started believing the things Hannah told her about Ms. Sandra. From Nadia's house Hannah went back home to her grandmother for the holidays and again left back for school after the holiday was over.

Hannah's report card was greatly affected with all the stress she was going through as a young girl, so her mother took her to her university and asked one of her male friends, a math teacher, to tutor her. This man, Peter, after a few days of normal tutoring started taking Hannah to his room, and he would be watching movies inappropriate for her age. Watching these movies reminded Hannah of the abuses she received in the past, and so she started shaking and crying. Ms. Sandra's friend, Mr. Peter, while watching this movie, came really close to Angel and started touching Hannah wrongly. Hannah tried to fight him but couldn't, so she just started screaming.

After approximately four hours, Hannah's mother came back and picked her up. Hannah did not bother telling her mother what had happened, knowing already that her mother did not care about her and her emotional pains. However, Hannah summoned the courage to tell her mother after that emotional pain she was feeling, hoping her mother would do something about it, but of course, she doubted Hannah and nothing more was done. These became the types of situations Hannah was thrown into by her own mother until Hannah left Nigeria for the United Kingdom (UK). Ms. Sandra would normally pick Hannah up in good emotional state from her grandmother and would bring her back broken in pieces, both physically and emotionally. She would come back to her grandmother emotionally broken, always in pain, and always having bloodstains on her clothes.

No matter how much Hannah cried around her own mother for the love she desperately needed, Ms. Sandra never supplied her any tender, loving motherly love she asked and wished for. It was as if Hannah was invisible to her mother because Ms. Sandra never really acted as though she saw her. Ms. Sandra only seemed to notice her daughter when she needs her to do something for her. Although Hannah was not a genius with her schoolwork, when it came to doing things for her mother, like washing her car, Hannah was always available and would do it immediately in an attempt to win her mother's love. She did everything possible to win her mother's love until she realized that nothing she could ever do for her mother would help her gain her mother's love though she is her mother's only child.

So Hannah started asking about her biological father even more whom Hannah heard was a respected lawyer in the United Kingdom. As Hannah's aunts visited a couple of times from there to see their mother, Hannah would write letters to her biological father, hoping for a reply.

However, Hannah's father, Mr. Jude, never sent a reply letter for Hannah through her aunts. However, she never gave up on him because she always trusted her grandmother's words, who informed her that her father loved her. Hannah just assumed that maybe her aunts couldn't get to him and therefore couldn't give him the letters or couldn't get the reply from him and therefore started giving the letters to everyone her grandparents knew were visiting the UK that knew her father, but still there was no response coming from him. This was the case for four years until Hannah finally came back to her birthplace in the UK on September of 1996 to complete the rest of her educational years.

Chapter Six

Coming Back to the United Kingdom (UK)

Coming back to the UK was one of the best yet the worst thing to happen to Hannah simply because Hannah now had the opportunity to move ahead with her education and career, and not to forget, she got to reunite with her big cousins and maybe meet her biological dad as well as her biological big sisters. Most of all, coming to the UK was a perfect way to get away from the pains her uncles caused her. On the other hand, coming back to the UK would keep her away from her grandmother as well as her loving friends. There was no one else there in the house to help her grandmother, Mrs. Grace, around the house but her irresponsible uncles. The thought of Hannah having to now live with her mom alone and not being able to have her grandmother around for consolation was not easy for Hannah to accept, but she had no choice. Hannah came, and the first place both she and her mom stayed at was her aunt's, Ms. Sandra's youngest sister, Lisa's, house with her husband and their two children, Tracy and Emanuel.

27

While living at her aunt's house, Hannah went to her other aunt's house, Charity and Brittany's parents' house, for a visit.

Reuniting with her big cousins, of course, would be an amazing moment to Hannah, being that they had not seen, spoken, or even written to each other for many years; so they were very excited and happy to reunite. From here, Hannah also got to meet her other cousins that she never knew, and they all went around their neighborhood. They took pictures, joked, and laughed together.

Something else happened in this house that was also a surprise to Hannah when she came to visit her big cousins.

While in their house, Hannah went to use the restroom and came out of the restroom screaming so loud and crying at the same time as she was confused, unknown to her what she witnessed. Everyone started asking Hannah what was wrong, but she didn't want to talk to anyone but her favorite cousin, Charity. And so she called her cousin to the restroom and told her of the blood she saw coming out of her. Hannah was sixteen years old. The month she came to the UK was the same month she received her first period. This also was a blessing to her because during those periods, she was going through all the rapes and molestations. Hannah could have gotten pregnant had her period started earlier or could have even caught an incurable disease when she could not fight for herself, but to the glory and mercy of God, she didn't start her period until she left her uncles and anyone else that could have gotten her pregnant.

After staying for a little while with her big cousins, Hannah and her mother went back to her other aunt's house where they were staying. From here, Hannah and her younger cousins started spending much time together and got to know each other very well. Having spent so much time with her cousins, Hannah became very close to them, especially her young female cousin Tracy. They had a caretaker for the children, and she was one year older than Hannah. Both Hannah and the girl would always go back and forth to drop and pick up the little cousins from school.

One day Hannah's mom came and asked her to get dressed up to go somewhere with her, and Hannah got dressed into what she wanted to wear. But her mother insisted that Hannah wear something different, and just that little misunderstanding caused an argument between them. Hannah told her mother to take her to her father and that she wants to go and stay with her father.

Before she could even put her hand on Hannah, Hannah called the police on her. Earlier that day, when Hannah was with her big cousins, Hannah told them how she was afraid of the way her mother treated her and how she used to beat her when things did not go her way, so they told Hannah about an emergency call number. They asked her to call that number if ever she should run into any type of trouble, and the police would come quickly to her rescue. Having this in mind, when Hannah's mom was about to beat her, she called the number and three police cars came in front of the house in less than two minutes. The police asked around what was going on. When they asked Hannah what happened, Hannah told them that she wanted to see her dad but her mother wouldn't let her. So the cops took Hannah to the police station. They asked Hannah her father's name, and she told them. They made phone calls, and in less than three minutes, Hannah's father came to the police station with his new spouse. This was Hannah's first time seeing her father, and this was his first time seeing Hannah; but he couldn't even say anything to her other than "how are you?" No hugs, no kisses, no I love you, but Hannah answered both him and his new spouse while still believing that he was the best father on earth based on what her grandmother told her about him and her two big half-sisters. Hannah's father then told Hannah that they would see each other again later, and then he left.

By this time, Hannah's mom was inside the police station waiting for her to finish with her dad outside. The same week, while still at her younger aunt's house, Hannah's mom spoke to her aunt and asked her to talk to Hannah's dad and set up a meeting with Hannah and her father. Days after the appointment was made, Hannah's father came and took her to his private office where they chatted and laughed until they both fell asleep.

After spending time together, of course, it was time to go their separate ways. He went to his new spouse and children while Hannah went back to her mom. But before Hannah left, he gave her one hundred euros and a little white dress for church, which Hannah wore not too long after their meeting.

After three months of staying in her aunt's house, Hannah's mom decided to move to England and took Hannah with her. Hannah then continued her education and enrolled into the high school, which was a great thing for her because it gave her the confidence she needed to strive for a better life. While in England, they stayed in one of her mother's female friend's house, who was married.

Although Hannah came straight from Nigeria, she found out that she was way much ahead of the other students with the curriculum they were being taught, which really lifted and encouraged her spirit. At first, she was afraid of fitting in with these new groups of students, but being ahead of most of them in their schoolwork, she was befriended by many of the students in order to get her help in tutoring them, especially in mathematics.

After living with her mom's friend's house for about three months, tension arrived since Hannah's mom, Mrs. Sandra, had no job at the time and the woman they lived with, having her own family and now Hannah and her mother to care for, felt so burdened. So Hannah's mom had another friend, who was a pastor, John, and married to Mrs. Alia with a daughter, Maria, who was about two years younger than Hannah. Mrs. Sandra spoke to the pastor and the spouse in favor to stay with them but only for a moment until she could find a job, and they allowed them both to come in with them. Maria went to the same school as Hannah was going to, coincidentally, although Hannah never met her, considering she was in a higher grade than Maria was and the school was big. They started going to school together and, moreover, walked back from school sometimes together. Of course, every gift not from God always has a downside to it, and coincidentally again, Hannah had to pay the price.

Hannah was very happy to be in this house because it felt as though she was in Nigeria again due to the way Maria and she played like two sisters.

From going to their church, Hannah's mom met another friend of hers, a single male, Mike, who shared a house with one of his male friends, James. She decided to leave Hannah with the pastor's family and move in with her male friends. Some days she would come by and take Hannah out for a visit to her male friend. After about five months of living with the pastor, the pastor's spouse, out of insecurity, insisted that Hannah and her mother leave the house. The woman of the house came back one day to find Mrs. Sandra in the house, which was unusual because she is normally home whenever Mrs. Sandra comes for a visit. Although nothing was going on between the pastor and Mrs. Sandra, the woman of the house felt some sort of insecurity when she came home and saw her there and therefore called Mrs. Sandra into a different room and spoke to her and asked her to take Hannah and leave their place.

After church that Sunday, they both moved in with Mrs. Sandra's male friends, James and Mike. The house had three bedrooms. Mrs. Sandra and her friend James shared one room. Mike stayed in the other one, and the last room was left empty for the guests while Hannah slept in the rug of their living room. Because their house was a bit far from the school, Hannah always caught the bus to the school. This meant having to wake up earlier than usual for Hannah, coming outside at certain time to wait for the bus, and standing there in the cold during the cold weather and waiting for the bus alone.

Most nights when Hannah would be sleeping, Mike would come out to the living room to watch TV and, in so doing, would wake Hannah up. And Hannah would just lie there as though she was still sleeping in order to avoid bringing any attention to herself. Instead, the following morning, she would go to her mom, and her mom would tell her to just manage, being that it was not their place. And just as she said,

Hannah would keep enduring with some sleepless nights and drowsy days since he would watch TV until he fell asleep, leaving the TV on.

To Hannah's knowledge, her nightmare of men abusing her wrongly was over because this was the longest Hannah had gone without being molested or raped. That was until one night, when Mike came out to watch TV. But instead of watching TV, he came to where she was sleeping and started touching her in a wrong manner, though he didn't do anything to her.

The following morning, he asked Hannah's mom permission to take Hannah to the park, and Hannah's mom agreed. He took her to a hidden place, an unfinished building (almost deserted), and started telling her that he loved her and cared for her. He knew at that age Hannah needed some attention—which she was not receiving from anyone else, including her own mother. As he was telling Hannah how much he loved her, she replied kindly and just stood there. He assumed Hannah would fall into his arms, but what he didn't know was the fact that Hannah had already planned to use him to get something that was important to her at the time. Hannah played along with him and used his cell phone whenever she needed to call her younger aunt in London. Both Mike and Hannah agreed to start a relationship, but to keep it from her mother. Hannah, to keep him from trying to sleep with her, told him that she was a virgin and planned to remain so until after marriage, so he never expected any type of sexual relationship from Hannah. What he didn't know was the fact that Hannah was using him for another plan. He always gave her money for anything she wanted even though she might not necessarily need it. Though Hannah was happy with the school part of her life due to the friends she had, everything else was not very suitable for Hannah there.

On one particular day, Hannah had an argument with her mom about something, and her mom got upset and picked up her shoe and threw it at Hannah. The heels of the shoe hit Hannah in the right wrist, and it got swollen. Hannah went to school and couldn't write or even move her right hand. Her friends and the teachers started asking her what happened, but when she tried to lie to them, they wouldn't believe her and, seeing the seriousness of the swell, threatened to have it reported to the superintendent and get an investigation done on it.

Hannah left the school immediately and called her younger aunt and told her what happened. Both she and Hannah didn't want her mom to get into trouble, so she went to the Western Union immediately and sent Hannah some money for a ticket to come back to her place. The next morning, when everyone left the house, Mike went with her to the Western Union and picked up the money and bought a ticket and left immediately. Before leaving, Hannah was told by Mike that he would come by and marry her, but Hannah didn't really believe him and didn't really care but, however, agreed with him just to get him to help her leave for London. To Hannah's surprise, about one to two weeks after leaving England, she received a certified mail from Mike, which was an engagement ring. Hannah's aunt went to sign for the letter and called Hannah to know whether to sign for it, but Hannah immediately told her to write return to sender; and she did so.

From that day, Hannah never heard of him or saw any more of his letters. Hannah's aunt told Hannah's dad, Mr. Jude, that Hannah was in there with her.

When Hannah's aunt found out that Hannah's mom was coming back and was looking for Hannah, she told Hannah's dad that she did not want Hannah's mom to find out that Hannah has been staying with her without letting her mom know, and for that reason, her dad asked Hannah to move into his house. And so it was that Hannah finally moved in with her father and his family.

THE MOVE TO HER FATHER'S HOUSE

Hannah was so excited to move in with her father not just to get to know her father better but also to know her brothers and sisters she never really met before and to finally get the chance to be with them. As Hannah's dad came with her stepmother to pick her up, all the excitement ran away when she saw the look her stepmother gave her. Hannah became so afraid of her due to the intimidation her stepmother placed on her.

Moving in with her father was one of the best things that could have ever happened to her not because of the experiences she learned while living there. Throughout Hannah's little time with her father before moving in with him, he never told her that he had other children from his current spouse. Hannah was surprised walking into his house and seeing his new children, three boys and one girl, totaling seven children her father had with three different women.

At the time of the move, the first child, a boy, was eleven years old. The second child, also a boy, was nine years old. The third child, a boy, was seven years old, and the last child, a girl, was three years old. They had a nanny, an old woman who stayed in their basement.

Surprisingly to Hannah, the same basement was the same place her father placed her while he and his other family members stayed on the second floor. Hannah's big sisters at the time were in the universities and were at the boarding school, and therefore, Hannah did not see them. Two months after the move, the two sisters came back from school for holiday, and there Hannah met with her big sisters. And the family hugged with laughter and joy.

Hannah was rather surprised because she received no love from her so-called family, including her two big sisters. Perhaps this was because she came there with high expectations of having a great and better life with them. Of course, not knowing about her father's new spouse and children pulled Hannah's hope low since Hannah expected to reunite with her two big sisters with the same love her grandmother told her they all had for her. But instead, she got there to see that whatever love they have had for her was only when she was an infant, and things have changed from what they once were. Hannah was always threatened by her stepmother because of the way her stepmother treated her. Apparently, her stepmother had in mind that Hannah moving to their home might be the key her parents would use to reconcile and get back together.

Hannah's stepmother did not work and never knew how to take care of herself physically. Her face was covered with pimples, and she was not very attractive and was, therefore, very insecure of Hannah's dad leaving her for Hanna's mom. What she didn't know, however, was the fact that Hannah was happy her parents where no longer together. Though most people would not understand, but Hannah saw it to be a blessing from God, especially seeing the way the children there in the UK lived their lives and the way most Nigerian children that were raised there also behaved in such an untraditional, dishonorable, and *disrespectful* manner. Hannah believed her parents' divorce was the one good thing that brought her back to Nigeria where she attained the respect, honor, integrity, morals, and the manners most of the children and teenagers lacked.

Hannah's stepmother treated her as though Hannah was her slave in the sense that she turned Hannah into her servant. She made Hannah do the work that her nanny would normally do with little to no pay to Hannah. Her big sisters went to a very good private high school in their city while she was enrolled in one of the worst public high school within their neighborhood. The only outfits Hannah had were the same once she brought with her, and these also became her school wears. Hannah, however, managed to make friends with popular students with tough brains. Under normal circumstances, Hannah would be what today's teenagers call a geek; but because she did really well in her courses, she was tutoring most of the popular students, which brought them really close to her. Unlike most teenagers, she loved going to school because that was the only thing that took her out of this house; and in school, Hannah had many friends that helped take away, most times, her stresses and depressions.

Her older sisters called their stepmom their mom, and when Hannah first moved in, her stepmom also wanted Hannah to call her *mom*; but Hannah refused. Rather, Hannah called her *aunt*—mainly because Hannah felt that though her own mother did not show her love, she was still her mom and was still alive. Hannah was raised very differently from the other children and believed her mother was the only woman she should call *mom* as long as she was still alive. Hannah also felt the word *mom* to be very special and is not to be used for everyone rather to those that have earned it or to their biological mothers, and Hannah felt that her stepmother has not earned that word yet. The following day, Hannah brought some pictures of her mother and presented it to her new siblings, and Hannah's stepmother told Hannah's other siblings privately that Hannah was one of the new servants to cover the truth that their father had another child outside their mother.

Hannah's stepmom was not threatened by her big sisters because their biological mom was dead, and they took her as their mother. And for this reason, they all got along very well. Whenever Hannah's stepmom was around, her big sisters would treat her as though they didn't care about her to make their stepmother happy. However, when the woman was not around, they would call Hannah to stay with them and their brothers and sister to fit in with them, but it was not the same for Hannah because it felt like they only did it out of pity and not out of love.

On one occasion, Hannah's brothers' friends came to the house for a visit and saw Hannah and asked them who Hannah was, and they replied and told him that Hannah was one of their servants. This was when and how Hannah found the truth and asked her dad, but both he and his wife pretended not to know why she was introduced as their servant.

On another occasion, Hannah was doing her schoolwork in the kitchen table where she normally did her schoolwork. The eldest son came to the table and talked to Hannah about being happy to be their father's first son, and Hannah replied by telling him that she was also happy to be her father's third daughter. That night, Hannah's stepmom came to her little room and asked her why she told her son that she was the father's child, being that they did not want the children to know that Hannah was also one of them. Hannah stared at her and said nothing to her, but when she left the room, Hannah started crying.

Next, Hannah went to her dad one day for help with her schoolwork. Though Hannah understood what the assignment was, she was looking for an excuse to spend time with her father. But before Hannah could ask him for help, he turned away and asked her to go to her stepmother. Hannah showed it to her, but when she couldn't figure out how to do the exercise, she said that she did not have the time to help her.

One day, when no one was home, Hannah's eldest sister brought her to a private location to talk to her. This was a good experience for her because she told her that she knew what Hannah was going through in the house. She told Hannah that she had to be strong and that Hannah could overcome all the circumstances she was passing through. This was one of Hannah's great days here because her stepsister made her feel as though she was not alone.

After two years of moving in with her dad, Hannah's mom started asking around for Hannah and found out that the father enrolled her in one of the worst schools in his neighborhood. She came there one day looking for Hannah, and to Hannah's surprise, Hannah was sparingly happy to see her mother for the first time in her life. Around the same time, she started coming to her father's house to request to reunite with her daughter; but of course, Hannah's father refused. Hannah's father knew that if Hannah went back her mother, then he would be forced to pay child support, which he did not want to do. Instead, he took Hannah to his lawyer's office and asked her to leave a statement to his lawyer about how bad her mother treated her while she was with her, but for some reason, Hannah did not. Rather, she told the lawyer that she would think about it and then get back to him.

When they got home for the first time, Hannah's father spent time with her in order to gain her trust; but of course, he did not know that he was setting himself up for Hannah's next question to him, which was "All the letters I wrote you while in Nigeria, why did you not reply to them? Did you not get them because my aunt said she gave them to you, or did you not love me then?" Of course, he denied receiving them with a guilty look on his face. He then told Hannah that he loved her and then asked her if she wanted to go back to her mother.

Hannah responded no, but that night she couldn't sleep because she kept thinking of the conversation she had with her stepmother about going to university. In that conversation, her stepmom came to Hannah's room that night to ask her why she wanted to stay with her dad as opposed to her mom, and Hannah told her it was because she wanted her dad to help in paying her school fees when she got to college, like he paid for her older sisters—having in mind that the other alternative to having her school fees paid would be taking loans because she knew her mother would not help her with it. Hannah asked her stepmom if her dad would still pay for her school fees if she stayed with her mom, and she replied to Hannah saying, "I guess that's the only reason you moved in here after all." From that response and with the look on her face, Hannah knew then that they would not help her either way.

The following day, Hannah went to her dad and told him that she had made up her mind to go back to her mother because she knew his house was too full for her. She then told her father that though he had no more space in his house for her, she hoped there would still be a little space left in his heart. He said okay and went and told his wife to inform Hannah to get her things ready to go back to her mother's place that month.

While in her father's house, Hannah kept a diary of both things that happened in the school and at home. She did not know that her stepmom, having no life, went to her room when she was not around to read her diary. On the diary, Hannah wrote things about the way they treated her and this guy she had a crush on in school. One day, Hannah was cleaning up the children's living room when her stepmother came to her and repeated everything Hannah had written in her diary. Hannah was so broken and couldn't say anything, so she just went to her room and cried. By the end of that month, Hannah had moved back with her mother.

CHAPTER EIGHT

STRONGER DAYS

By this time Hannah's mom now has her own permanent place, a one-bedroom condominium in a very quiet neighborhood, and she was about eighteen years of age, going to her last grade of high school. When she moved in with her mother, she was able to reunite with her big cousins and the rest of her family from her mother's house that lived there in the UK. Hannah witnessed the big change that her mother had with everyone in the big family. Growing up with Hannah's big cousins, they never got along with her mother due to the way she treated everyone in the family, especially Hannah and her grandmother. While she was away, she managed to find comfort in Hannah's cousins and her sisters, and they became very close to the point that both Hannah's cousins and her mother's sisters sometimes came Hannah's mom's to cook for her, and her eldest cousin, who rarely spoke to her, came to Mrs. Sandra for comfort. Hannah was very happy with this because she got to be with her big cousins almost all the time, which was very uncommon due to when she was staying with her before, Hannah's relationship with her cousins was affected because of her mother's treatment toward them.

They all had much fun together, and Hannah felt as though things were perfect as they used to be back in their grandparents' house with her cousins. Her cousins, especially Charity, who was also her best friend, came there almost every day to take her around the neighborhood. She introduced Hannah to her boyfriend and most of her friends. Hannah's mom was a teacher and would only have time to cook for them on weekends. Whenever Hannah's cousins came over, she would offer them something to eat, and sometimes, her cousins would jokingly say to her, "I don't want to eat your Monday or Tuesday food," depending on the day of the week. These were the only days that Hannah saw a different part of her mother together with her family. When Hannah found out that her big cousins were working, she decided to get a job too for the first time, and she applied to so many places. Luckily, she found a job that kept her busy most times when she is not in school.

Being that Hannah's mom just arrived and did not have much money saved and needed some money—she went to Charity's father and borrowed some money. After a few months, Hannah's mom got a joy but at the time was still unable to pay him back, so they started having problems. Charity's dad was particularly upset because he felt that by that point, Hannah's mom should have paid him back. Again it started affecting Hannah's relationship with her cousins that they barely saw each other as they used to, and sometimes her cousin Charity would sneak in to spend time with Hannah. They both knew that no matter what, they were sisters and best friends, and nothing could take that away. When Hannah's mom found out that Hannah was still close to her cousins and their family, Hannah and her mom again started having problems. Mrs. Sandra always found any little reason to call the police on Hannah and have her taken out of the house, and sometimes Hannah would go to her younger aunt's house. Hannah was already uncomfortable with what her younger aunt told her mom and Hannah when they first came to their house. She told them that her husband was acting weird because he didn't want them in their house. Hannah's mom called the police on her so many times, and each time she went to her younger aunt's house that her aunt's house became her first home. Her aunt had a problem with alcohol, which nobody in her mother's family believed until Hannah started going to her house very often. Each time Hannah went to her aunt's house, her husband would always give Hannah a negative vibe, and when she ask her the reason, her aunt would tell Hannah it's because he didn't want Hannah in their house.

One day Hannah received the courage to ask him why he didn't like her, and to her surprise, her uncle revealed the secret of her aunt being a drunk to Hannah. He explained to her his reason for his attitude, which was that his wife was a drunk and her mother's family is not doing anything to help her. After talking with him and having seen her aunt several times when she's drunk, Hannah started talking to her about her problem and how it's affecting her family, especially her two little children. Hannah made it her responsibility to involve the rest of the family in her aunt's problems. At first the family didn't believe Hannah because her aunt would lie to her sisters and her friends about her problem. Hannah's aunt, being angry with her for telling her family about her alcohol addiction, began a rumor that Hannah was trying to steal her husband and her family from her. Some people started believing her, being that Hannah was almost in her aunt's house every day due to the problem she now had continuously with her and how often her mother would call the police on Hannah. Unlike most teenagers in our current days, Hannah found no thrill in hanging out much with friends after school. Hannah didn't drink, smoke, or confide in teenage boys or males, which left her alone and with nowhere to go but her aunt's house until it became too unbearable for Hannah to handle. However, she managed to hang in there with her mom even with the troubles till her second to last grade of high school, after which she moved out.

Hannah decided to move into a homeless shelter about fifteen miles from her high school. Due to all the stress and constant depression, her school grades started slipping. While in her father's house and when she first moved in with her mother, Hannah was making good grades and received two honor roll trophies. Hannah was not making good grades like she was making, and her teachers noticed the difference in her through her face and sadness. Hannah was no longer focused in her classes in the sense that she no longer answered questions or worried about being the first in class every day. Her teachers, having observed the changes in her attitude and behavior toward the class, recommended that she spoke with the school counselor. Hannah spoke to her and told her all that she was passing through. Through all these, Hannah was still struggling with her job and school while taking several buses to get around.

Her mom came to the school and asked the principal and the counselor to tell Hannah to come back home but Hannah refused. She continued to disturb them until they begged Hannah to please go back home with her. Having only a few weeks before Hannah's graduation, Hannah went back to her mom while Hannah's counselor helped her apply to universities. When the letters came back, she was accepted in two great universities. Mrs. Sandra did not want Hannah to go to one of the universities due to the distance from her place. However, since one of the colleges was very far from her place, she chose to take that one to get some rest from everybody, and Hannah's mom had no choice but to agree. Hannah's school counselor looked at Hannah and pitied her while crying and told Hannah to hang in there.

CHAPTER NINE

COLLEGE TIMES

Now Hannah was away for college and far from her mother and all the stress she was passing through, although all she wished patiently for was for things to get better for her emotionally, that way her grades couldn't be affected. Hannah studied prelaw her first year mainly because her mom had already implanted it into her head. Hannah grew up in a place where being a doctor and a lawyer or being married to one was very significant. With that being the case, Hannah's mom, being a PhD holder in biochemistry and having married to a lawyer in the past, was so adamant about Hannah studying prelaw after Hannah personally refused to study medicine. Hannah was able to find a job while in college and worked throughout her time in college to keep herself busy when not in class.

Before coming to this school, Hannah's mom took her dad to court, and the court, after hearing both sides, proposed that Hannah's dad would pay 71 percent of Hannah's school fees while her mom would pay the remaining 29 percent. This was a private college and, therefore, was more expensive than the average federal universities. The fee per semester was up to $18,000 plus, but with the grants and financial aid, it comes down to about $11,000 plus. Hannah's mom would prepare the estimated amount Hannah's dad is supposed to pay and then send it to him. When she prepares the estimated amount, she would exclude the financial aid and the grant, and after Hannah's dad pays his share, there would be about extra 2000 Euros left. Hannah's mom would end up not having to worry about paying anything, and this was the case throughout Hannah's years in college.

During Hannah's second semester, her mom dropped Hannah off to school, and from there, Hannah met her roommate, Eunice. One of Hannah's biggest fears happened when her mom took her roommate's phone number and continuously harassed her until she eventually got tired and dissociated herself from Hannah. Although it was not her intention to chase Hannah's friend away, that was always the outcome. Hannah loved her mom and always listened to her advice, although Hannah might not do what she advised her to do in the order she tells Hannah to do them. Mrs. Sandra got so insecure, being that Hannah was her only child, and if she thinks Hannah was taking Hannah's friend's advice as opposed to hers. Due to her insecurity, she tried her best to push everyone around Hannah away. First she pushed away Hannah's dad and her siblings, then Hannah's aunts and uncles, and finally Hannah's close friends.

Just as Hannah feared, her mom took Eunice's number. Mrs. Sandra started harassing Eunice. Being in college, there are some days Hannah didn't have classes and other days she had late classes and, in those days, would not have to wake up early. The same case applied to Hannah's roommate, who rarely went to her classes, but rather goes out with her friends and always comes back very late at night, at which time Hannah would already be asleep. Mrs. Sandra was a high school teacher who wakes up very early in the morning to get ready for her classes. Whenever she woke up, she would call

Hannah's room line. Hannah, being fully aware that it would be her mom, would tell Eunice not to pick up the phone; however, Mrs. Sandra would continuously call the room line or Eunice's number until she picks up. Eunice had so many discussions with Hannah concerning Hannah's mom and her early morning phone calls being a disturbance to her. Hannah tried many times to talk to her mom but never succeeded in getting through to her mother. When Eunice tried talking to her, Hannah's mom took it as an insult but never changed her ways.

Going off to college for Hannah was to be a way to run away from the stress and related family troubles and problems, but instead Hannah ended up going to different counselors, hoping to get rid of the entire emotional breakdown from both childhood and adulthood trauma that were boiled up in her mind and heart. After going to many counselors, they all gave Hannah one solution, which was talking to someone she believed to be the course or source of the fear, anger, and pain within her. Finding out the solution to Hannah's emotional breakdown would be very difficult, being that her emotional breakdown was not just from those she knew but also from those she did not know back in her childhood. On the other end, Hannah believed there was nothing she could do about it, considering the only person she really blamed for her problem was her mother and there was no way she could get through to her.

Hannah, believing that she could not talk to her mom, was advised by her counselor to talk to her and find out her mother's reasons for all the traumas and pains her mother put her through. However, after a few months, Hannah received the courage to ask her mother what she's done that made her treat Hannah so badly, though she's her mother's only child, and her mother replied and told Hannah that she was not fond of Hannah because Hannah was her only child, and not only did Hannah come from her father, but Hannah also looked just like him.

Now Hannah knew for sure that nothing she could ever do would change her mother's feeling toward her because Mrs. Sandra's reasons were unchangeable, and this became Hannah's life situation throughout her times there in college, but as the Word of God says in Zechariah 4:6, " 'It's not by might nor by power but by my spirit,' saith the Lord of host." Hannah, throughout her tribulations there even in college, still passed through and graduated five years later.

CHAPTER TEN

THE VISITATION

About two years before Hannah's graduation from college, her grandmother came for a visit. She stayed at Hannah's younger aunt's place for two weeks, after which she went to Hannah's older aunt's house where she stayed very briefly.

It was over three weeks when her grandmother visited, but Hannah was in school and for that has not seen her grandmother. However, two months after the visit, Hannah was off school for the Christmas holiday, and she came back to her mother's house where she would be able to get to her aunt's house and see her grandmother. Being that Mrs. Sandra and her sisters were still not getting along, she prevented Hannah from going to her aunt's house even to visit her grandmother. Hannah begged her continuously to permit her to see her grandmother, being fully aware that if she left without her permission even at her age, her mother would not hesitate to call the police and have Hannah taken out. This became very difficult for Hannah because she wanted to spend the holiday with her grandmother but did not want to stay in her aunt's house since her aunt had already started spreading news that Hannah was after her husband and family.

Hannah explained to her mother in a very low voice that she missed her grandmother and wanted to see and visit her and spend Christmas Day with her. Hannah tried to make her mother understand that she needed to see her grandmother, having not seen her in so long, but Mrs. Sandra insisted that Hannah must not go; so Hannah told her mother that she loved her and respected her but she must go and see the woman who raised her with so much love, and nothing would prevent her from doing so. Hannah, after speaking with her mother, left her mother's house, waited for the bus on that freezing snowy day, and from there went to her aunt's house to see her grandmother.

When Hannah arrived at her aunt's house and saw her grandmother, they were both happy to see each other after so long. They hugged and shed tears of joy together. They started talking, and Hannah asked her about her best friends back home and their neighbor. She replied that everyone was doing great, and they laughed and took pictures together. Hannah's grandmother asked her about her father, and immediately Hannah started crying.

Even at her age, Hannah couldn't hide the pain and agony she passed through when she stayed with her father and his family, so Hannah told her how badly both her father and his family treated her. Hannah looked at her grandmother, and she could see the pain in her eyes. So Hannah told her that she was very happy because no matter how badly her parents treated her, God was there with her both emotionally and physically, and her grandmother was so happy to hear how strong Hannah was. Hannah's grandmother told Hannah not to worry because she was going to talk to Hannah's father and let him know that he has disappointed Mrs. Grace.

In less than two hours after Hannah's arrival to her aunt's house, Mrs. Sandra arrived as well, screaming and yelling at her sister for letting Hannah into her house. Hannah's mom was more concerned with taking Hannah, being there that she didn't even care about seeing her own mother. Hannah's grandmother witnessed what was going on and talked to Mrs. Sandra. She said to her, "My first child, even at your age, you have not left your stubbornness behind." Hannah's mother said nothing; rather she went inside and stopped yelling.

The following day, Hannah's grandmother insisted that Hannah call her father's house, and Hannah did as she requested. Immediately Hannah's father picked up the phone and knew who it was talking to him. He handed the phone to one of his family members, and the person pretended as though he didn't know who was talking and took a message for Hannah's father.

Hannah's grandmother, after talking with Mrs. Sandra before Mrs. Sandra left, decided to move in with Hannah and her mother. Around that first week of January, before Hannah went back to school, her grandmother moved in with them, and Hannah was thrilled, happy, and excited for the first time to stay in her mother's house, knowing that she would no longer be alone.

In less than two weeks after Mrs. Grace moved in with her daughter, both Hannah and Hannah's mother had to go back to school. Hannah moved back to school, and her mom started teaching again. Mrs. Grace, not knowing her way around the place and not having anybody to take her around, was always home by herself until Mrs. Grace and Mrs. Sandra agreed after two weeks that it would be best for her to go to Hannah's older aunt's place where there would be other children that would always be in the house to keep her company.

Hannah's uncle-in-law (older aunt's spouse) was not very fond of her grandmother due to an unsettled argument between him and Hannah's other uncle-in-law in Nigeria. Her older aunt's spouse took out his anger on Hannah's grandmother though Mrs. Grace never sided with either of them. Hannah's uncle-in-law became very bitter toward her, and this led to a bad relationship between Hannah's grandmother and her uncle-in-law and made it difficult for Hannah's older aunt to give her mother the full attention she needed. Hannah's grandmother, not getting the full attention and having just arrived from Nigeria in a different atmosphere, started having some health problem. If you asked me, I would say it's true. The Bible says in Genesis 2:24, "A man shall leave his father and mother and be joined with his wife, and the two shall become one flesh." I don't believe the Bible was implying that one should abandon his or her family, however sad to say, but this is exactly what is happening today in our world. Mrs. Grace was not abandoned by her daughter while in her care but, however, was neglected, especially being an elderly in need of attention, tenderness, and care.

Mrs. Grace decided to move back with her younger daughter, and from there her health condition only got worse, not getting the medical attention she needed; and she was taken to the hospital where they discovered that she was severely malnourished and her only way of survival was through a pacemaker, which was then implanted in her chest.

You could imagine how this whole incident affected Hannah emotionally when she heard how things were with her grandmother. Hannah decided to move to a school closer to where her grandmother was staying. She started slacking even further on her schoolwork and went late to her job several times due to her constant visit to the hospital.

After Hannah's grandmother was released from the hospital, Mrs. Sandra took her to her house, and they both agreed that Hannah would be coming by to check on her grandmother whenever her mom was at work. The surgery that was performed on Mrs. Grace made it very difficult for her to fully help herself. Some days Hannah would go from school to work and then to her mother's place to check on her grandmother and feed her. Other days Hannah would sleep over at her mother's house to keep her grandmother company and then take the bus to school the following day. Mrs. Sandra, due to the misunderstanding she still had with the members of her family, disconnected every member of the family from her, with the exception of Hannah. Charity, Hannah's cousin, was too fond of their grandmother that she could not stay away from her grandmother. Hannah tried her best to call her cousin whenever she was with her grandmother, knowing how much her grandmother loved Charity as well. However, Hannah had to limit the calls since she could only make the calls with her cell phone, and with the pacemaker on Mrs. Grace, Mrs. Grace is not supposed to be around electronic devices.

Some days, when Hannah's mom would be at work, Hannah would sneak Charity in the house to spend some time with their grandmother, and it really made Mrs. Grace very happy to see her.

One faithful afternoon, Mrs. Sandra was in the kitchen cooking while Mrs. Grace was in the living room massaging her feet in warm water and then had a stroke. Mrs. Sandra immediately called and had her rushed to the hospital. Mrs. Grace was treated and, to the glory of God, survived but could no longer walk and could hardly chew and swallow.

She was released from the hospital, and Hannah decided to stay home more often. The doctor showed the family some therapy that could be used in helping her walk again, and they started using those therapies on her. In approximately one month, she started doing so much better on her own and started walking in slow pace again through the glory of God. They still had to take care of her daily needs in bathing her and cleaning her up when she goes to the bathroom and so forth.

During her next regular checkup at the hospital, the doctors said she was doing much better, but they wanted her to stay a couple of days for them to do some test on her. At the hospital, she stayed in bed for the duration of her hospital visit, and that affected her walking capabilities yet again. Being that she was just recovering from a stroke, she needed constant therapies to help her, which she was not getting from there. She came back home unable to walk or talk, and she was no longer able to help herself with basic needs.

During this time, the doctors suggested to them that it would be better if she were put in the nursing home, considering the family could not provide her the necessary attentions she needed twenty-four hours a day, seven days a week, and that's exactly what she needed in case of an emergency.

Hannah's older aunt and Mrs. Sandra still refused to put their differences aside to help their mother, and almost every day, Hannah would call her aunt begging her to put everything aside for the sake of their mother; but both her and Mrs. Sandra were very stubborn and could not agree with each other. Hannah and Hannah's mom still continued to help her grandmother with her therapies and her daily needs. Not long after Mrs. Grace's incident, she ended up in the hospital again, and everything went downhill from there, being that while in the hospital they didn't help her with her therapies and she couldn't talk much to the workers in the hospital. After several visits to the hospital, Mrs. Sandra decided to take her mother to the nursing home, where they all believed she could get better.

Being that Hannah was in school and was working at the same time, this was taking much of Hannah's time having to visit her grandmother, go to her classes, and go to her job. After a week, Hannah went to the nursing home to see her grandmother and, from what she saw, was not happy at all due to her grandmother's conditions. Though while in the nursing home she started talking and was getting better drastically, she still was not walking even with the therapies she was getting.

The last time Hannah came to the nursing home and saw the pains her grandmother was in due to the treatment and emotional confusions she also went through. Hannah went back to her campus, knelt down, and prayed her first payer to God that came from her heart. As the Word of God said in John 3:16, "For God so loved the world that He gave His only begotten Son, so that whosoever believeth in Him should not perish, but have eternal life." She prayed, "Dear God, please take my grandmother away from this earth. She deserves to be with you where she would be happy and in good health. I promise if you take her with you, I would spend the rest of my life worshiping you. Thank you for answering my prayer. Amen."

This was a very big sacrifice that Hannah made because she loved this woman very much and believed she had no one else but her and wanted her grandmother to live there with her. After this prayer, Hannah got up and cried for about three hours, and all she could think to herself was there was nothing in this world that she could give her grandmother that would come close to what God would give her in heaven.

After two months of treatment without receiving any good news, the family stopped paying the nursing home, and two weeks later, Hannah's older aunt was contacted by the nursing home to come and take their mother. Hannah's aunt, without telling anyone, took Mrs. Grace back to Nigeria, and in her condition, her body needed much rest and could not handle the strain she received from the travel. Two days after her arrival to Nigeria, she passed away.

<h1 style="text-align:center">Chapter Eleven</h1>

Graduation Period

Normally, graduating from any level of education, especially college/university, is very exciting, but Hannah's case was very different because instead of getting her things ready for graduation, Hannah cried all the time. Not just because she missed her grandmother, but when she remembered how much she loved her and how much pain her grandmother went through before she passed away, it was much for her to handle. She always remembered how her grandmother taught her many things that the children around her lacked, such as morals, respect, integrity, honor, hope, faith, and most of all, love. It's a shame how people quickly forget the pain and suffering one goes through for them.

Hannah's graduation year was so hard because besides being emotionally broken, she had to pass all her courses and bring her GPA to a certain level for graduation. This was the same years that

Hannah's mom and her aunts went back home for the burial of their deceased mother.

Hannah's cousin Charity and Hannah made up their mind not to go home for the burial because as much as they loved and cherished their grandmother, going there would bring back a lot of memories that they both believed they couldn't handle.

Beginning of the next year, Mrs. Sandra and their sisters went home for the burial, and Hannah agreed with her mother to move back home for that last year due to the expense. Right before Hannah's graduation, she lost her job for being consistently late and for not doing her assigned duties well. Now Hannah had no job and had bills to pay so applied for unemployment benefits while looking for a new job. With the unemployment she was receiving $550 a month, and with some money left over from the loans she took in school, Hannah was able to pay for the $500 a month for five months and pay for her phone bills. She stayed there and finished her last semester of university and then started looking for jobs and finally found a job working with a lawyer in a courthouse. With the money she was making, Hannah was able to buy a car, and her mom agreed to insure it together with Mrs. Sandra's other two cars, which would mean putting the car under her name.

Through all of Hannah's tribulations, she received her driver's license and—to the glory of God—was able to endure all and graduated with her bachelor of arts degree in sociology and pre-law.

All along, Hannah believed she was just lucky to have found a wonderful job, but something amazing happened at this job that convinced her that it was God himself that brought her to this job. Within three days of being at this job, Hannah met an amazing woman of God, Ms. Brianna, who God used to bring Hannah closer to God. Out of the respect and honor Hannah was raised with, she called this woman auntie because she played a role of not just a friend or even an aunt but a mother as well.

One day Hannah started discussing with her about the mother she had and how tired she was of dealing with the stress. In that conversation, Hannah mentioned to her that she no longer believed in God because he let her grandmother die and let Hannah suffer all these. After talking with Ms. Brianna, the woman told Hannah losing her faith in Christ does not solve the problem but adds more tribulations to her life, and from there Brianna invited her to her church, which Hannah started going to.

Hannah started driving her car back and forth to everywhere, from school, to church, and work. And one day, on the road her car had a problem, and she did not have enough funds to take care of it. Ms. Brianna assisted Hannah with the bills in repairing the car. Hannah's mother came back the following day and discovered that the car was not parked where it's normally parked at. She asked Hannah where the car was, and Hannah explained to her the problem with the car and that the car was still at the mechanic being taken care off. Hannah's mother became very furious when she discovered that Hannah didn't go to her own mechanic but rather went to a different one and, out of curiosity, wanted to see the car. Hannah explained to her mother that a very good friend took Hannah to her mechanic who was fixing the car. Hannah's mother stopped by Hannah's job and insulted both Hannah and Ms. Brianna, who in the process of getting all kinds of insult from said nothing but stared at Mrs. Sandra until she finished and left the building. Ms. Brianna looked at Hannah and apologized for the wrongs Hannah's mother had done and sympathized with Hannah and her situations.

When Hannah's mother first came back and saw the changes in Hannah's life, at first she was so impressed and happy since Hannah refused to go to church with her before she left to Nigeria but was now always in church.

After two weeks of her arrival, she became fed up with Hannah being in church all the time. Now instead of complaining to her friends that Hannah was an atheist, she complained to the same friends that Hannah went to church too much. Hannah rarely fought with her unlike the usual; instead, whenever Hannah heard her coming home, Hannah would pick up the Bible and start reading.

Hannah started seeing a big difference in herself and became very serious with the work of God. Every member of the church loved Hannah to the glory of God—especially the pastor, who was so fond of her. Now being very close with the pastor, Hannah decided to tell him a little bit about her mother's abuse toward her, and Hannah told him how her mother harasses everyone that comes close to Hannah. The pastor assured Hannah that he is not like everyone else that runs from Hannah's mother and that he being a true man of God can handle Hannah's mother and her harassment.

One of the pastor's sons, Joshua, found an interest in Hannah in less than five months of knowing, and they started talking privately and she started telling him some of the things she went through back in Nigeria. He also told Hannah his painful stories of abuses he received as a little child. Being so close to Ms. Brianna, Hannah told her the interest Hannah had in this boy. She advised Hannah to pray and ask God to take control, which Hannah did.

Mrs. Sandra tried so hard to pull Hannah away from this church and when she couldn't, she started harassing her good friend Brianna, but to the glory of God, Hannah's friend, knowing all about Mrs. Sandra, didn't let Sandra's harassment push her away from Hannah. Instead it brought them closer. This became very frustrating for Ms. Sandra that she started finding faults in everything Hannah did in the house. Eventually one night, Hannah was sleeping, and Mrs. Sandra woke her up and got into an argument with her and then called the police and asked them to remove her from her house as usual.

Usually, Hannah would be scared, but this time Hannah felt some sort of comfort and happiness that she couldn't explain. Hannah kept hearing it all over in her spirit what she could not explain. She called her good friend Brianna and some members of the church, but there's no answer. So Hannah called one of her other friends from work and told her what happened, and she immediately sent her husband to come and pick Hannah up. This was how Hannah finally moved out of her mother's house after so many years of endurance.

The next morning, Hannah called her cousin Charity, who has been living with her boyfriend, and told her what happened. Charity came and picked her up to stay with her and her boyfriend. After staying with them for about two weeks, Hannah's good friend helped Hannah in finding an apartment in Brianna's complex.

CHAPTER TWELVE

FINALLY MOVING OUT

The following month, Hannah moved into her own apartment, and in the same complex lived not just Hannah's friend Brianna but another family member of the church, Samson, with his wife, Mercy, and their three children—their daughter, Christy, and two boys, Michael and Ken.

Before Hannah's mother moved to Nigeria, Hannah added her mother to Hannah's phone plan because Mrs. Sandra messed her own credit up with the phone companies and couldn't get a plan without any other way. Hannah was paying the phone bills by herself but could no longer pay the bills on her own having her rent to pay. Mrs. Sandra increased her harassment on Ms. Brianna, hoping to push her away from Hannah. While living there, Hannah developed a very strong relationship with Mrs. Mercy and her family, and Hannah's mom did not know about her at the time and therefore did not harass her. However, with all the harassment Brianna was receiving from my Mrs. Sandra, Brianna was still very close to Hannah. Hannah learned many things while she got closer to God, and one of them was the difference between worldly friends and those friends you have in Christ and that they would stand by you and pray with you.

Hannah's friends from work, knowing what emotional pain she was going, encouraged her to go back to her father and start a new relationship with him but to keep it from her mother. They explained to Hannah that maybe her father wanted nothing to do with her because he knows that her mother was in her life.

After trying so much to push Hannah's friend away from Hannah without succeeding, Mrs. Sandra started coming to Hannah's church. Hannah was now living on her own and so didn't have to see her mother anymore, although her mother constantly called her. Whenever Mrs. Sandra would come to Hannah's new church, Hannah would become afraid of her mother because she did not want her mother to destroy this relationship Hannah now had with these new church members. Hannah's friends would see the fear in her face whenever her mom came there in search of her, and they would later tease her due to the way Hannah would talk around them with such pride and then run whenever she saw her mother.

Mrs. Sandra, finding out how close Hannah was to the pastor and the fact that the pastor was ignorant of the person Mrs. Sandra truly was, used the pastor to get through to Hannah. The pastor, out of ignorance, gave his cell phone number. Mrs. Sandra introduced herself to him. This would be one of the biggest mistakes he would find out in the future he ever made. Hannah's mom called to set up a meeting between herself, Hannah, and the pastor. At first, Hannah was against it, but the pastor managed to persuade her come to the meeting. Hannah didn't really say much during that meeting, so with Hannah's pastor being a father assumed her mom was only acting out of her concern for Hannah's future. The pastor believed Mrs. Sandra's heart to be that of a mother who only came by to make sure all was going well with Hannah. Hannah became very upset with him for believing her mother's lies but later understood that it wasn't his fault and accepted that he was just ignorant of the truth of who her real mother was. The pastor also found out that Hannah's mom was a very good friend of one of his elder brothers from school, which made it even more difficult for Hannah to convince her pastor of what type of person her mother was.

Within eight months of being in this church, the pastor's son that Hannah found an interest in, Joshua, proposed to her and accepted due to her feelings for him. Although this was one of Hannah's happiest days, Hannah could not get excited because she didn't really know how to get excited. They became very close and started sharing many secrets with each other. For the first time in her life, Hannah experienced a different type of love, and it felt really good to her. Hannah loved that feeling so much and did not want to let her mother know, in order not to lose it. They both agreed to keep the engagement from her mom for the time being because of the type of person her mother was. While Hannah was after love, tenderness, and care, her mom had already informed Hannah of the type of man she must marry, which was either a doctor or a lawyer.

Though Hannah didn't care much about reuniting with her father, she felt she had to because of her fiancé, and both her fiancé and Hannah agreed that it was time for her to not only reopen her relationship with her father but also to let him know about her engagement. And from that month, Hannah started trying to get in contact with him by going through one of his good friends, who was also a reverend father.

Hannah's good friend Brianna was one of her father's clients, and she gave Hannah his office phone number and office address; and Hannah started searching for him. And one day Brianna was on her break from work and volunteered to take Hannah to her father's office with Mercy's spouse in the car with them. They got there, and Hannah started shaking; but they prayed with her and asked God to take control.

Hannah went in his office and left a different name for the receptionist in case he didn't want to see her. He called her in, and she went in and greeted him as she sat down in one of his chair. He asked her why she used a different name, and she replied and said she did so in case he wouldn't want to see her. And she told him she needed to talk to him. Hannah informed him that she had tried several times to contact him without success, and he replied and asked her what she wanted with him. From that response, Hannah really started crying and told him that she came to give him an update on her life and to tell him that she was engaged. Hannah also told him that she wanted to know if he would walk her down the aisle for her wedding, and he asked for her mom. But to make things better between them, Hannah lied to him and said she has not seen or spoken to her mother since she graduated. He asked Hannah how she was doing, and she told him all was well with her.

Hannah's dad at the time told her she did not want anything to do with her because she chose to stay with her mom. Hannah, in tears, got on her knees and apologized to him for hurting him. He hugged her and told her that he had accepted her apologies, and then he asked Hannah if she really loved her fiancé. Hannah told him she was confused because she was not sure if she was only with him due to the loneliness and emptiness she felt in her heart or if it's really love. He then asked Hannah what qualities Hannah desired in her husband, and Hannah told him. He asked her if he had those qualities and she said yes. Then he replied, "Well, if you truly believe he loves you, maybe you should wait and find out if you really love him before making this decision. As far as being there for you, I would be there for you when you need me. After all, you are my child." Hannah thanked and hugged him and then told him that she would call and come to visit him whenever she could.

From that day, Hannah tried much to keep in touch, but whenever she called and left messages with the receptionist, she never got any response back; and sometimes his wife would come with him to work, and she would take the calls and maybe not give him the messages or persuade him not to return Hannah's calls. One day Hannah called before they came to work and left a message on his answering machine. When he returned Hannah's call, she informed him that she had been calling and leaving messages, but he told her he never got them. After trying so hard to keep in touch with him without succeeding, unless

Hannah called so early and left a message, Hannah stopped, and he never called her back.

Being that the job Hannah had was a temporary job and was only for a year, Hannah had no job and no other way of survival.

Chapter Thirteen

JOBLESS BUT HOPEFUL

ow Hannah had no job yet had many bills to pay for. Beside her phone bills, Hannah also had to worry about her light and apartment bills as well as other bills. Mrs. Sandra knew Hannah lost her job and would need assistance in many ways. She used this opportunity to find a way to bring Hannah back to her and therefore started calling Hannah very often. Due to the pains Mrs. Sandra had caused Hannah in the past, Hannah did not believe her mother was calling her out of love, and therefore ignored her calls. Mrs. Sandra tried many ways to separate Hannah from her new friends but couldn't find a way, so she started spreading lies to all of Hannah's friends and her own sisters that Hannah was prostituting in her new church to pay her bills as a way of survival, being that Hannah lost her job. To the glory of God, these people that she said these things to knew very well what Hannah was capable of and therefore did not pay much attention to Mrs. Sandra's words. They told Hannah all that her mother was saying concerning her, but even then Hannah refused to

65

take her calls, knowing that Mrs. Sandra told all those lies only to get Hannah's attention. When Mrs. Sandra still couldn't get that attention, she called the pastor, begging him to set up another appointment for three. After refusing many times, the pastor finally agreed and set up the appointment.

They had the meeting. At the first eye contact with her mother, Hannah said nothing to her. They both sat down, and the pastor asked Hannah if she had anything to say. Hannah immediately asked her mother what she had called the meeting for, and Mrs. Sandra responded that she wanted to help Hannah move forward and advised Hannah to go to nursing school. But Hannah did not pay attention to her mother's advice. The pastor asked Hannah why she did not want to follow her mother's advice, and immediately, Hannah started crying and replied as she continued crying, "Who has a mother like mine that would do everything to ruin my image? My mother went around spreading the types of rumors that any loving mother would hear and kill somebody for starting. How can a loving mother tell her friends that her only child is a prostitute?"

As Hannah was still speaking, the pastor stopped her with this shocking information with a surprise look in his eyes and asked Mrs. Sandra if what Hannah said was true, and Mrs. Sandra said yes and said she believed that would have been another option that Hannah used to survive since Hannah had no job and still made it through without Mrs. Sandra's help. The pastor gave Hannah napkins and replied to her mother, "Mrs. Sandra, I have only known this girl for a few months now, but I can vow for her that she is not that type of person. Unlike most adults in her stage, she's not interested in males, nonetheless being a prostitute." The pastor then told Mrs. Sandra the he had been assisting Hannah in ways he could all these while and immediately asked Mrs. Sandra to apologize to Hannah. Mrs. Sandra apologized and then asked Hannah how she paid all her bills, and Hannah then told her mother that she just filed her taxes and is also receiving unemployment. Mrs. Sandra advised Hannah to become a substitute teacher if she did not want to go for nursery school. Hannah explained to both the pastor and

Mrs. Sandra that she had already tried for nursery school but couldn't afford the expenses and that she does not think she could handle being a teacher. After all was said, the meeting finally ended, and they all went their separate ways.

The pastor loved Hannah so much and started talking to his son about getting married. Unknown to the pastor, Hannah and his son, after spending much time together, realized that they were not made for each other for Hannah noticed the pastor's son was very controlling and never listened to her. She also noticed that he was also very lazy and would rather stay at home and watch TV all day as opposed to going out and doing something with his life and spending some time with Hannah. He, on the other hand, felt as though Hannah was too needy because she always wanted to spend time with him. Trying to make things work between Hannah and Joshua, Hannah went to Brianna and asked her for help. This became a big snare to their relationship because he felt as though instead of talking to him, she ran to another woman, and he took it as an insult. Hannah tried to explain to him, but it only went downhill from there until they finally brought their case to the pastor. And the pastor, after hearing both sides, helped them reconcile.

A month later after their reconciliation, Hannah's unemployment was finished, and she had little to no money left to pay off her bills. Hannah was unable to pay for her next month's bill and had no other way of surviving except either getting another job or taking any possible wrong path to make it. Hannah started making a few calls from some jobs she found on a newspaper and called the number for a position she saw and was given an interview for the following day. Hannah went to the main office and was given the full detail of what type of job it was, and it was an enrollment to join the military. Hannah, being desperate for help but with no one to help her, felt as though she had no choice and, for that reason, decided to join the military, which came with bonuses and benefits. Hannah agreed to join the army without talking to anyone but her fiancé, his family, and her friends Mercy and Brianna from the church about it, knowing already her mom would not support her. Hannah came to the church with the paper she received from the office stating the job qualifications and the pay, and she showed it to her fiancé, her two great friends, and the pastor. They all encouraged her to take the chance as they prayed for her, letting her know that they would always be by her side for love and support.

The following day, Hannah's mother called her continuously until Hannah eventually took her call. Mrs. Sandra asked Hannah to come by to see her and take some assistance from her, but Hannah told her that she had found a job and did not need her assistance at the time. Mrs. Sandra asked what kind of job it was, and at first, Hannah lied and told her mother that it was a federal office job in a different city from their current location. A few days before Hannah left, her friend Mercy delivered their bouncing baby boy.

While on the plane to go to her training location, before the plane took off, Hannah called her mother and told her the truth that she joined the military and was on her way to the training area located in a different city.

CHAPTER FOURTEEN

WHAT? JOINING THE MILITARY?

Can you imagine a daughter of a lawyer and the other a PhD holder in biochemistry joining the army as a way to survive? This of course was her only option and the only job Hannah could find in the short time she had to find a job before becoming homeless. Although Hannah's mother claimed to the world that she made much money yearly, yet her only child had to run to the military as a way of survival. The army seemed like the perfect opportunity for Hannah to start over and fight harder without family distractions.

The ending of that year, Hannah left for Paris, for the army combat basic training. Hannah's mom started, of course, harassing Hannah's friends and the pastor by blaming them for Hannah joining the military. Joining the army was one of the best things Hannah did for herself. Although the trainings were very hard and difficult for her at first, being away from her friends and families were even harder. However, she learned to be more independent and to believe in herself as well as to work with different groups of individuals with different beliefs. The trainings taught Hannah a lot, most importantly on how to manage her hours.

Hannah woke up daily at 5:00 a.m. for their daily training on weekdays. After waking up, they would leave for their morning exercise, which is called PT. This PT would last for about one to one hour and a half, after which they would go and eat breakfast, which would last about twenty minutes—sometimes less, depending on where they had to go next. After breakfast, they would go out to the field on weekdays or clean up their rooms and the front of the building on weekends. Hannah only had the opportunity to use her phone on weekends to reach her family and friends.

Beginning of that December, Hannah had a two-week break and went back home to visit her friends and families. You would think Hannah has had it bad so far, but her trouble and her tribulations never seemed to leave her sight. Hannah came back only to enter another hell on earth because Mrs. Sandra, no matter what, never ceased to amaze her daughter with Mrs. Sandra's ways of harassment. Mrs. Sandra blamed Hannah's friends for helping Hannah move into her own place before joining the military and blamed them for Hannah running off to the army and therefore hated them with passion.

Every day from that, when Hannah would go to her church, Mrs. Sandra would call the pastor and continuously harass him and his family. Hannah visited the pastor for a few days and all hell broke loose, and her mother called and cursed at Hannah, the pastor, and his wife. Mrs. Sandra threatened to report the pastor and his family to all the Nigerians back home and tell them that the pastor was running a prostitution club instead of a church, and of course, that really got to the pastor's skin, which anyone could understand, although Hannah knew that Mrs. Sandra was just making the threats to the pastor to push them away from Hannah. Hannah's friend Brianna kept telling Hannah to do something about Mrs. Sandra and advised Hannah what to do concerning this issue. Mrs. Sandra, of course, had her motive for everything she was doing, and the reason being that she found out that Hannah was in a relationship with the pastor's son. Mrs. Sandra did not support this relationship and tried all she could to destroy it. Mrs. Sandra had already found this doctor she wanted Hannah to marry. Hannah's mom discovered that the pastor's son had no job and was neither a doctor nor a lawyer. Hannah's mother told her about the doctor she found for her, but Hannah told Mrs. Sandra that she was not interested; and for that matter, Mrs. Sandra started harassing the pastor to keep away from Hannah, and when she did not succeed in pushing the pastor away, Mrs. Sandra lied on another end to the pastor that Hannah was already in another relationship with one of her doctor friends. The pastor, out of confusion, did not know what to believe and what to do. Can a mother lie against her own child? This was the pastor's question. Though Hannah was not happy, however, she did not blame the pastor for giving Mrs. Sandra the opportunity to tell him. Hannah was on the bus from the station to the campsite when her cousin called her and told her what was going on with the pastor and Hannah's mother. Hannah called the pastor several times and, after ignoring her phone calls, eventually picked up, and Hannah tried to apologize to him for the harassment he received from her mother and assured him that Mrs. Sandra was lying. But the pastor wouldn't let Hannah finish, and he told Hannah that he knew the devil was using her mother to try to divide Hannah and him from being very close, like father and daughter. Hannah was very relieved to hear him say that but still called her mother and warned her to quit the harassment.

When Hannah got back from the vacation, she had about three weeks to graduate basic training, and two weeks after which, she arrived and something very unbearable happened that almost took Hannah back to her road of isolation. Hannah's best friend Mercy, who had always showed Hannah true love, told Hannah that she wanted nothing to do with Hannah anymore. Every Sundays when Hannah had the privilege to use her phone for at least three hours, she would call her best friend Mercy first. From the first day Hannah was introduced to Mercy, they both got very close and took each other as big sisters and best friends. Mercy was very good to Hannah, and Hannah was also attached to Mercy's little son, Michael, who loved Hannah so much and was not happy when Hannah left off again to the military. They all loved each other and became one happy family. Hannah loved him so much mainly because he loves to hang around her all the time, and that was something Hannah was not used to. Hannah was used to rejections as opposed to being loved as much by the little boy, and his family loved her. She made sure to call her friend Mercy before calling anyone else in order to speak with her young son.

On a particular Sunday, Hannah called her friend Mercy only to receive one of the biggest shocks of her life. Mercy told Hannah that she and her family wanted nothing to do with Hannah anymore because a friend of Mercy told Mercy that Hannah's mother was a witch and was using Hannah to get through to Mercy and her family. At first it didn't make sense to Hannah. She could not respond and rather kept quiet. Mercy told Hannah never to call her family again and that if Hannah didn't heed to her warning, she would report Hannah to the pastor. Mercy then hung up, and Hannah started reliving her years of being unwanted or rejected. Hannah called the pastor for consolation, but because it was a Sunday, the pastor did not pick up. She called his wife in tears, and she answered. Hannah could hardly get her word across because she was crying but managed to tell her what happened. Knowing how close to Mercy Hannah was, the pastor's spouse advised Hannah not to worry about anything and that she would talk to Mercy for Hannah and find out why she spoke to her in such manner.

Although to most people it would make sense why Hannah would care so much that Mercy wanted nothing to do with her, but because Hannah was already so broken about many things, it was just becoming too much for her to handle all at once. The kind of treatment Hannah was receiving from this army training camp, the way things were left between Hannah's mother and Hannah, and the fact that Hannah's mother was already trying to ruin the only relationship Hannah had ever had was becoming more than Hannah could handle at all at the same time.

Hannah called her fiancé to tell him what happened, but he didn't take her calls. Now Hannah became very worried and confused, but in less than twenty minutes, Hannah's time with the phone ended and she had to give back the phone to their training leader. Hannah's friends started asking Hannah what was going on, but she just said nothing and kept crying. Talk about tribulations upon tribulations, but all Hannah can do was cry while still reading her Bible, believing God would help her somehow get through these times, which of course he did because Hannah was still moving on.

Being that most soldiers held their phone, Hannah also kept her own and tried over and over in that night to get through with her fiancé, but he would not take her calls. With all that was going through, Hannah assumed he no longer wanted her and stopped trying. Beginning of the following year, Hannah graduated from basic training and left to a different city for her job training.

One of the major differences from basic training and her job training was the fact that they were allowed to keep their phone always, although they were not allowed to use it at certain times. For instance, they are not allowed to take the phones while in classes; they are not allowed to use the phone when they are supposed to be cleaning up their buildings, and they are not allowed to use the phone after the lights-out, when they should be in bed.

Having her phone always was a good opportunity for Hannah to call back home and talk to her fiancé and her parent-in-law-to-be. Hannah called her fiancé the first day she arrived, and he picked up. She started crying to him and told him what happened between Mercy and her, and he started laughing and asked Hannah if that was why she was crying. He then assured Hannah that everything would be okay and that Hannah should not let it bother her at all. However, he asked Hannah if Hannah was interested in dating the doctor that her mom wanted Hannah to marry, and Hannah could not understand why her fiancé would ask her that. Hannah told him that she loved him and was not interested in marrying any other man than her fiancé. They left that conversation like that and got off the phone after talking for a little while.

The following day, Hannah called him all day, but he didn't take her calls. She believed that something was wrong, but the other part of her wanted to believe that her fiancé rejected her calls because he was in church all day. Hannah called the pastor for over a week, and the pastor rejected her calls and did not return Hannah's calls.

Hannah became very concerned because she was afraid that something bad might be going on between the pastor's family and her mother, who might cause a problem between Hannah and her fiancé. Hannah texted the pastor and expressed her concern on the text message. The pastor finally returned her calls and apologized for being too busy, and Hannah told him that his son was no longer taking her calls. He assured Hannah that he would talk to her fiancé, but he also informed her that his son might have backed up because of her mother. Immediately the pastor hung up with Hannah. She called him right away to tell him something that just came to her mind, but the pastor didn't pick up; so Hannah left it for him on a text message.

After three days of calling her fiancé without any response, Hannah called the pastor. But he also didn't take her calls as well. She called her friend Mercy, hoping that her mood had changed because she also is very close to Hannah's fiancé, but she picked up the phone and rudely hung up after warning Hannah never to call her house again or else she'll report Hannah to the pastor. Hannah called for another week and received no response neither from the pastor nor his son. Hannah decided to leave them voicemails and thanked the pastor for being a father to her and told them she understood that Mrs. Sandra, her mother, was a pain to them. Hannah also told the pastor that she completely understood if they wanted nothing to do with her due to her mother's harassment on them. Lastly, Hannah told him that she saw it coming, considering Hannah and Mrs. Sandra's family all ran away from Hannah in order to avoid her mother's harassments. Hannah stopped calling anyone and just stayed on her own for about two months when her fiancé called and asked her if she had been talking with the guy her mother wanted her to marry. Hannah was so upset and asked him to tell her what he really called for. He told Hannah that he saw the guy that looked prettier, and he thought Hannah should give that guy a chance. Immediately Hannah started crying in a very low voice, realizing that he called really to break up with her. Hannah asked him if she had done something wrong to him, and he said no. Rather he said Hannah's mom was more than his family could handle. Hannah asked him if he spoke to the pastor, his father, and he said yes and told her that both he and the pastor came to the conclusion that their relationship would be better left behind. Hannah expressed to him that she was disappointed in him because she believed his family to be true born again Christians. He asked Hannah why she would say such a thing, and Hannah replied and said because true born again Christians would know temptation when they see it. Hannah told him that her mother was a key the devil used to break up a relationship ordained by God, but clearly he and his family couldn't see that. Hannah accepted the rejection, and he begged Hannah to understand and to forgive him for not being able to handle; and Hannah agreed.

In a way, this was one of the best things that truly happened to Hannah because she saw herself closer to God than ever, reading the Bible more than before, crying and travailing to God more than before, and getting stronger and stronger. However, Hannah felt alone and very empty, with no one but God to turn to or talk to. She did not attempt calling anyone from that church for at least one and half months, and no one from that church, including the pastor, called Hannah until around the end of next month. Two weeks before Hannah graduated, Mercy needed something from Hannah and asked her husband to call Hannah and ask her if she could help her, although her husband never called Hannah back since she told him what went on between her and Hannah, but anyway, Hannah agreed, being a true woman of God.

By the end of the month, Hannah graduated from training and was on leave to go home for a break. Hannah stayed for extra two weeks plus and went back for a position in a different country. Hannah was transferred to South Korea two weeks after her break. Before moving, while arriving home for her break, Hannah's mother came to the airport to pick her up. Hannah stayed in New Jersey with her mother and called neither her friend Mercy nor the pastor and his family, except for her ex-fiancé but in order to keep the promise she made to her friend Mercy through him. A week after Hannah came back, she made an arrangement to meet with Joshua, her ex-fiancé, for help in delivering something to her friend of which Hannah promised Mercy already. Hannah met and ex-fiancé and talked for a little bit at a restaurant, and before Hannah left, she bought a friendship card and put five hundred dollars ($500) in it and asked him to please deliver it to Grace when they meet next.

Hannah managed to call the pastor's spouse the same week she came back because she was always good to Hannah. Hannah came to inform her that she was being transferred overseas to South Korea on an assignment. The pastor's spouse expressed that she was going to miss Hannah.

The following day, the pastor called Hannah and asked her why she had forgotten him, but Hannah told him that she did not forget him, rather the pastor forgot her. The pastor asked her to come by for a blessing prayer from him before traveling to South Korea. Hannah told him that he really hurt her by not being there when she needed him. However, Hannah left the house immediately and went to see him.

As Hannah got to the church, everyone hugged her with many excitements. She greeted them all and then went inside the church and saw Michael, Mercy's husband, who was very close to her, and his big sister and younger brother Ken. All the children in the church came and hugged Hannah. She was very happy to know that they all missed her as much as she had missed them, but Hannah went straight to the pastor's office to see him. He was in a meeting with somebody, but the minute he saw Hannah, he ended that meeting and hugged her for a very long time. He asked Hannah how the training went, and she told him everything was a success through the glory of God. He then asked Hannah what happened, and she told him everything, from the breakup to what happened with Mercy and her. Hannah told him that she was not happy the way things went with them and her. He assured her that he did not support the decision with his son for the breakup and still believed Hannah was meant to be his son's spouse, but he son was too blind to see it.

The following afternoon, Hannah came by the church with some of her graduation pictures to give everyone. The pastor and Hannah talked for a little bit, and she left. But before she could leave, the pastor asked her to come back again that night because they had night vigil till the following morning, and Hannah did so. That night, Hannah told Mrs. Sandra that she was going to see the pastor and she got dressed only to come out and find out that her mother had hidden the key from her. From that situation, Hannah could not go and informed the pastor that she would not be able to see them but would come by on Saturday morning before she catches the plane, which would leave at 8:45 a.m.

On Saturday morning, Hannah took the train and came by the church and hugged everybody good-bye. Hannah promised the pastor that she would try to call them whenever she got to South Korea, which she did the minute she arrived and had the chance to call. On the day Hannah was leaving to a foreign country she had never been before and knew nothing about, she left being very upset at her own mother. How much healthier can this relationship get before either one of them permanently loses each other?

Chapter Fifteen

Last Thoughts

ooking back to those years, you might not understand, but I believe it to be a great blessing when one passes through trials and temptations. God let Hannah go through the heartache and brought her out of them in order to use her to show that he is always with us. The Word of God says in 1 Peter 1:6–7, "Where in ye greatly rejoice, though now for a season if need be, ye are in heaviness through manifold temptation: That the trial of your faith, being much more precious than of gold that perished, though it be with fire, might be found unto praise and honor and glory at the appearing of Jesus Christ." I believe today that with God's power, tender loving-kindness, and mercy, we all can go through anything and still come out without a scratch. The Word of God says in Isaiah 43:2, "When you pass through the waters, I will be with you; and through the rivers, they shall not overflow you. When you walk through the fire, you shall not be burned, nor shall the flame scorch you."

I believe Hannah was afraid and was too young and too ignorant at first to know much about God, but he was there with her every step of the way, both in good times during her childhood in the village with her grandparents and the times she shared with friends and in bad times. The Bible says in Deuteronomy 31:6, "Be strong and of good courage, fear not, nor be afraid of them: for the Lord thy God, he it is that doth go with thee; he will not fail thee, nor forsake thee."

The following are questions with an advice answer:

1. Are you tired of waiting for the answer?
2. Have you lost your faith, are losing your faith, or never had faith due to afflictions and tribulations?
3. Are you thirsty for spiritual growth? Disappointment?
4. Have you ever been alone, worried, and discouraged with no one to turn to?
5. Do you need peace, strength, and love?
6. Are you having marital problems?

If you answered yes to any of these questions, then, please, this next chapter is for you. Let these quotes help you acquire more understanding about life and what it brings. I have experienced most of these life situations with no one to show me how amazing God could be but God himself. Most of us today are lost because we never had anyone to show us the way. Just like God delivered Hannah, so would God guide you through that destiny the Almighty has written and prepared for you even if it would take you through several difficulties. Please use this quote to help you not only to have courage but also to let God be your strength.

I went through my abuses and almost took my life, but to the glory of the Almighty Jehovah, who was my guide, I understood somehow that this life does not belong to me but to him who created me. Just as the Word of God says in Colossians 1:16, "For by him all things were created: things in heaven and on earth, visible and invisible, whether thrones or powers or ruler or authorities; all things were created by him and for him." I am for God and God alone. Nothing would turn me against him and him against me. God's love for me is all I need to get through life.

Unlike Hannah's fiancé, her families, her friends, or even my own families and friends who claimed to know love, God's love for Hannah was undeniable and cannot be divided, and the same goes for you. The Word of God says in John 3:16, "For God so loved the world that he gave his only son that whosoever believes in him should not perish but have everlasting life." The Word of God says in 1 Corinthians 13:4–6, "Love is patient; love is kind. It does not envy, it does not boast. It is not proud. It is not rude, it is not self-seeking, it is not easily angered, and it keeps no record of wrongs. It always protects, always trust, always hopes, and always preserves. Love never fails." The Word of God also says in Solomon Chapter 8:6–7, "The fire of love stops at nothing; it sweeps everything before it. Flood water can't drown love; torrents of rain can't put it out. Love can't be bought; love can't be sold-it's not to be found in a marketplace."

Although we have confused ourselves with the idea that love hurts, we have been deceived of the true meaning of love. Hannah's fiancé loved Hannah when he thought she was perfect, but real love stays and fights with you through thick and thin. Real love brings caring in spite of circumstances. Real love stays with you in times of problems and situations. This is the kind of love you give to someone even if they don't deserve it. The Bible tells us that God loved us and died for us while we were still sinners. In Romans 5:8 said the Word of God, "God demonstrates his love towards us, in that while we were still sinners, Christ died for us." This is what real love is. Hannah's mother only loved Hannah when it benefited Mrs. Sandra, but this is not what real love is for real love stays with you even without benefit.

As you read these quotes and many others in the Bible, I pray that you take a look at yourself and love who you are because God loves you. When you believe the lies of your mother, father, boyfriend, girlfriend, fiancé, or even your spouses have fed you and then realize later that these are lies, understand that you are human and therefore are inevitably going to make mistakes. God knows you before you were born and therefore knows the right spouse for you. Let God guide you as he has guided Hannah in making the right decision for yourself, but know the truth that God is by the door of your heart knocking for you and would not force himself in without your permission. Open the door for God, and go to him for help. He who created you would surely give you that which belonged to you when you follow and hope and trust in him.

Chapter Sixteen

Encouragement and the Word

1. Are you tired of waiting for your answers?

We go through so much in life that we wonder if God is still alive or if God is still with us. Having experienced firsthand most of these crucial life experiences, I must tell you that God is forevermore. Waiting on him is hard when you don't know if he sees you, but please, no matter what, don't ever give up. Wait and wait and wait patiently, for his time is the best. He is faithful and would answer at the appointed time. As you follow the ways of God and obey his commandments, wait and hope on him as he guides you. For the Bible tells us in Psalm 33:20, "Our soul waits for the Lord; He is our help and our shield." In Psalm 37:34, "Wait for the Lord and keep his ways. He will exalt you to inherit the land." In Isaiah 40:31, "Those who hope in the Lord will renew their strength. They will soar on wings like eagles; they will run and not grow weary; they will walk and not be faint." In Habakkuk 2:3, "For the vision is yet for an appointed time; but at the end it will speak, and it will not lie. Though it tarries, wait for it; because it will surely come, it will not tarry." In Hebrews 10:35–37, "Therefore do not cast away your confidence, which has great reward. For you have need of endurance, so that after you have done the will of God, you may receive the promise: for a little while, and he who is coming will come and will not tarry." In Hebrews 10:23, "Let us hold fast the confession of our hope without wavering, for he who promised is faithful." In Hebrews 3:14, "We have come to share in Christ if we hold firmly till the end the confidence, we had at first." As you read these passages, also look at Psalm 38:15, Isaiah 64:4, and Jude 21. Let these chapters in the Book of Life shape your ways of thinking concerning your hope and waiting on the Lord. God taught me through afflictions in order to use me to show you as he has shown me. Maybe he has as well chosen to teach you through afflictions or maybe other means. Please listen to the word, meditate on it, and let it be your guide. Never give up on the Living God, our Lord Jesus Christ, because he has not given up on you. For the Bible says in Romans 5:3–4, "We can rejoice when we run into problems and trials, for we know that they are good for us-they help us learn to endure and endurance develops strength of character in us, and character strengthens our confident expectation of salvation." The Bible also tells us in Proverbs 14:12, "That there is a way that seems right to a man, but in the end, it leads to death." Before you try to do it your way, think about the consequences and let the Bread of Life guide you because your way might not be the way of God, and your way could lead you through more afflictions and tribulations than you can imagine.

2. Have you lost your faith, are losing your faith, or never had faith due to afflictions and tribulations?

Welcome to Hannah's world before she met her savior, our Lord Jesus Christ. As Hannah often wondered during certain periods of her life, she wondered if God really existed and sometimes doubted God's goodness especially when it felt as though God wasn't hearing or answering her prayers. Then God himself reminded Hannah of how the serpent planted a doubt in Eve's mind concerning him. As he said in Genesis 3:5, "God knows that in the day you eat of [the fruit] your eyes will be opened, and you will be like God, knowing good and evil." God reminded her of the fact that Satan tempted Eve and succeeded in persuading her to believe that God was holding out on her and not giving her something good, which was more knowledge.

As a true born-again Christian, as you read this book, please reconsider if you're thinking about leaving your faith for any reason. Always remind yourself that your circumstances are the instrument used to measure atmospheric pressure of God's love and goodness. When you win the battle of faith, you win the world, and by doing so, you overcome any and every temptation the enemy might bring your way. Never forget that your faith is your shield, your virtue, and you can only stand upright with your faith. In this story you would see how impossible it would be for Hannah to explain the pain and agony she went through during this time.

It sounds so much easier and endurable reading it than it was enduring it. The molestations this girl Hannah received as a little child tormented her till, she met God, and through his grace and mercy, today Hannah can sleep peacefully without nightmares. When you are not sure, believe in one thing, and that is the fact that Jesus Christ is always there. When the going gets tough, when the ride is too hard, when it seems as though you have lost it all, always remember that Jesus will still be there. Your trouble, situations, or circumstances never changes our Living God. Please believe me when I tell you that the only way is through *God*.

The Bible says in John 15:4–5, "Abide in me and I in you. As the branch cannot bear fruit of itself, unless it abides in the vine, neither can you, unless you abide in me. I am the vine; you are the branches. He who abides in me, and I in him, bears much fruit; for without me you can do nothing. If you abide in me, and my words abide in you, you will ask what you desire, and it shall be done for you." In Revelation 3:20, the Word of God says, "Behold; I stand at the door and knock. If anyone hears my voice and opens, I will come in to him and dine with him, and he with me." The Word of God in John 14:6 says, "I am the way the truth and the life. No one comes to the father except through me." Please, my dear brothers and sisters, do not be deceived that there is any other way. Open the door, for God is knocking to you right now through; and if your door is not open, God is using this book to teach you that he is the God of impossibilities. *Jesus Christ*, the Living God, the I am the I am, the beginning and the end, the savior of the world, the author and finisher of our faith, only through him comes hope, joy, peace, happiness, and everlasting rest. The only question you need to ask yourself as you read this is, are you lacking hope, joy, happiness, peace, and rest? If so, then open the door and accept my *God*, our Lord Jesus Christ, who is the Living God, into your life.

3. Are you thirsty for spiritual growth?

Through spiritual growth many are now able to recover all that they have lost while in the world. This is your time, and God is here to lead you. What is the meaning of *spiritual growth*? When one grows spiritually, one becomes closer to God and hungers for God. When we hunger for God, the Bible says in Lamentations 3:23 that God proves to be good to the man that passionately waits and to the woman that diligently seeks him. The Bible also says that God satisfies the thirsty and fills the hungry with good things. When you are hungry for God or are seeking spiritual growth, much of worldly material pleasures become of less significance to you; however, all that you need and want is always made available to you. The Bible says in Deuteronomy 4:29, "But if from thence thou shalt seek the Lord thy God, thou shalt find him, if thou seek him with all thy heart, and with all thy soul." In the world today, we work for money and other material things. As little children even till adulthood, we do things for our parents, families, and friends, even strangers, in order to receive some type of reward. Why not grow in Christ and inherit the land and everything therein? In Psalm 107:9, "For he satisfieth the longing soul, and filleth the hungry soul with goodness."

As you read this, please don't let the devil deceive you with lies as he tried with me and failed miserably. As the Word of God says in 1 Peter 5:8–9, "Be sober, be vigilant; because your adversary the devil, as a roaring lion, walketh about, seeking whom he may devour: Whom resist steadfast in the faith, knowing that the same afflictions are accomplished in your brethren that are in the world."

As you follow this path of spiritual growth, let God and God alone be your guidance. Pray without ceasing and have faith in him. Understand that you are not alone in this quest because God and his faithful chosen servants or prophets are with you. You are now a different person; you are now our brother/sister. Please always remember that God is nigh unto all them that call upon him in truth. Psalm 18:10 says, "The name of the Lord is a strong tower; the righteous run to it and are safe." May God be your guide and bless you as you have chosen this path and as you continue to grow spiritually in the Lord.

4. Have you ever been or are you alone, worried, and discouraged, with no one to turn to?

Though as you read this book you would not understand the work of God with all the tribulations and difficulties in life, going back you realize that the best days of Hannah's life were when she felt alone in the world because those were the days when God taught her what no one else knew how to teach Hannah. Though she did not know God and therefore could not call on him for help, God took his place in fighting for her and saved her out of difficulties children, teenagers, and young adults could not get out off on their own. She fought hard to succeed through the right path in every tribulation she went through.

The Word of God says in John 14:18, "I will not leave you comfortless: I will come to you." Does that mean he only comes when you call him? No. He also comes when you need him but don't call him because there would be time when you do not know that you need him. For instance, growing up, when I was a little girl, I was forced to go to church every Sunday. I didn't know the importance of God or why I was going to church, and I did not know he could help me out of the physical pains I was receiving from people. Just as Hannah received all the abuses from many and still made it through even without calling on God, I didn't call him, but he still came and not only got me out my own difficulties in life just as he did for Hannah. The same way, he can also do it for you.

Just as the Word of God says in Psalms 18:29, "With my God I can leap over a wall." As long as you remember these words, you would never let any situation or circumstances discourage or separate you from serving and being with your God. Love for God brings faith, and through faith comes patience, strength, integrity, hope, grace, peace, joy, and much more than you would need to make it through in this world.

When it's hard, call on his blood, for this is the blood that purifies the body and cleanses sins. He took over Hannah's battle when all hope was gone, and he *can* do the same for you. Just remember that there is strength in the blood, and when you call on him in times of need, he would answer. God is the blood of the torment that washed away sins. He is the blood of the covenant, and he has promised to pass over whenever he sees the blood.

Before you give up on the Living God, first travail to God for help in filling you up with the grace of the holy cross because this is the grace, we all need. Ask the Divine Fire to come into your life because we live in the flesh, and we need the double portion of God's anointing especially when it comes to the restoration of your faith. God hears you; he understands your weakness, and with your faith, trust, and your heart, God will surely answer you at the appointed time. After all, the Bible tell us that by strength shall no man prevail, which means God is aware of the weakness of the flesh, and God, being the ultimate burning fire, would give us the strength we need to overcome any temptation. God understands that flesh and blood cannot do his will without grace. God also understands that without grace, there would be no righteousness, and righteousness is required for his work to be accomplished. The Bible says in Matthew 5:3–4, "Blessed are the poor in spirit, because the kingdom of heaven is theirs. Blessed are those who mourn, because they will be comforted." Stay in the blood and be free. As for me, I will abide in the blood of Jesus, for the Bible tells us that all those who abide in the conquering blood shall see the Lord; and that is the destination we are all fighting for. Many are called but few are chosen, and I have chosen to be part of the few. What about you, do you want to be part of the rejected many or part of the chosen few?

5. Do you need, peace, strength, and love?

If you answered yes to this God's special gift, then this is the time to open the door to our Heavenly Father. The Ancient of Days has promised to grant us our heart's desire. He who has promised never fails, and those who have tasted his greatness testify of his great reward and everlasting fulfillment, strength, love, and peace.

The Bible tells us in Romans 5:1, "We have peace with God through our Lord Jesus Christ." If God planned for us to have peace and the abundant life, then the question remains. Why are most people today not experiencing this life? The problem we have is faith and trust. We have failed to trust and have faith in the Living Bread. Our unbelief is our downfall today, for without belief, there is no faith; without faith, there is no righteousness, and without righteousness, there is no holiness. The Bible tells us in Hebrews 12:14 that without holiness, no one will see the Lord. This, in essence, means when we are filled with unbelief, which normally comes from the enemy, also known as the devil, we then lack peace because faith produces peace. In the following Bible verses, God helps us understand that we have peace in him. Psalms 37:4 declares, "Delight yourself in the LORD and he will give you the desires of your heart." In Psalm 107:9, "For he satisfies the thirsty and fills the hungry with good things," and in John 6:35, Jesus declared, "I am the bread of life. He who comes to me will never go hungry, and he who believes in me will never be thirsty."

When it comes to love, God had shown us his love in so many different ways. God had demonstrated his love to us in that he died for us while we were still sinners. The Bible tells us in John 3:16 that "God loved the world so much that he gave his only begotten son, that whosoever believes in him should not perish but have everlasting life."

What more can a father do for his children in order to prove his love than to give his life? God tells us that he has loved us with an everlasting love and has therefore drawn us with loving-kindness. In Romans 8:38–39, the Bible confirms the love of God to his people, saying "for I am persuaded that neither death nor life, nor angels nor principalities nor powers, nor things present nor things to come, nor any other created things, shall be able to separate us from the love of God which is in Christ Jesus our Lord." Are you looking for love? God is love and would never divert from loving you. However, in order to receive or experience the love God has given you as a gift, you must love him, which means accepting him as your Lord and savior.

6. Are you having marital problems?

If you paid close attention to this story from the beginning, you will see that the tragedies of this life started with the bad marriage the parents had. Developed countries such as the United States of America have destructive culture that makes it rather difficult for most married couples to make it. Read more of the Word of God and learn not to take that role of empowerment given to women in most developed countries if you're a woman. A negative effect only comes when a woman in a married relationship is fighting to play the role of a man when married because it only increases chances of destructive marital outcome.

When we talk about the wives in relationships, just like Hannah's mother, Mrs. Sandra, most women in our days regard their spouse as nothing when they are capable of working and making their own money. Most women in developed countries such as the United States of America have substituted the word of man for the Word of God. They do not understand the fact that it is only a privilege for a man to allow his wife to work for a living. The laws of man if opposite from that of God would surely die, for the Bible says heaven and earth may come to an end but the Word of God will never die.

If you compare some first-world countries that chose to live by the laws of men and some of the third-world countries that chose to live by the laws of God, you would see a big difference in their marriages and their divorce rate.

However, when we talk about the men of the houses today, most men make it impossible for their spouse to live in peace with them when their spouse gives them total control of their home. Most men refuse to understand how uneasy it is for a woman to stay home and care for their home as opposed to going off to work and making money daily. Although the men go out every morning to work and finish in the evening, they however need to understand that a woman's job is never complete. From morning to all through the night, the spouse is always at work. Men need to understand that even though the women are not working outside of the home, a woman's job is more hectic and more complicated than that of their men.

For those men out there who, after reading this, disagree with it, please, here is an experiment for you. For the next four weeks to six weeks, trade places with your stay-at-home woman. Let them go to work while the men stay home and care for the children and the home. The men must do all the chores in the house, which include cleaning the house, making sure there is cooked food in the house, helping the children with their homework, doing all the laundries, clearing the sink, etc. Ask your wife what she normally does in the house and do everything in the house that she does. As for the wife, she must do all the chores the husband usually does, which include going to work every morning and at the end, coming home to a cooked meal. Let your husband tell you what he normally does at work, and take over for him for this period of time. If this changes your opinion and attitude toward your wife and her chores in the house, then you are faced with a big decision, which is to mend or to break your family.

Are you having marital problems? Do you want all the problems, disagreements, and arguments to come to an end? Do you want to save your marriage from ending up in a divorce? There is a simple solution, and that solution is to live by the laws of God and not that of man. The laws of God can only produce happiness, joy, and a peaceful marriage while the laws of man can only produce bitterness and misunderstanding in the marriage, which can only lead to a divorce eventually or an unhappy marriage. The Bible says in Ephesians 4:22–23, "Wives submit to your husbands as to the Lord, for the *husband is head of the wife*, as also Christ is head of the church."

For a woman who wants to fix her marriage or live by the laws of God, simply play your role as a woman, just as God intended for you, even though your husband may not be playing his role. Obey and submit to your husband regardless of his wrongs to you. The Bible tells you to submit to your husband; however, does that mean a woman shall disregard the Word of God if that should be her husband's wish? No.

The Bible tells us to always do that which is right and acceptable to God. When a godly wife is doing that which is expected of her by God but her husband is not doing that which is expected of him by God, let her go to God in prayer without ceasing, and let God carry her burdens and solve her problems for her. You can only help your husband in two ways: first, talking to your husband with love and then going to God if your husband refuses to hear you. In Peter 3:1–6, the Bible says, "Wives, likewise, be submissive to your own husbands, that even if some do not obey the word, they, without a word, may be won by the conduct of their wives, when they observe your chaste conduct accompanied by fear. Do not let your adornment be merely outward— arranging the hair, wearing gold, or putting on fine apparel—rather let it be the hidden person of the heart, with the incorruptible beauty of a gentle and quiet spirit, which is very precious in the sight of God. For in this manner, in former times, the holy woman who trusted in God also adorned themselves, being submissive to their own husbands, as Sarah obeyed Abraham, calling him Lord, whose daughters you are if you do good and are not afraid with any terror."

Understand that you are privileged to be a wife and not a husband because you are not required to make any difficult decision but only help your husband in taking care of your home. I know it is difficult for a wife to obey and submit to her husband when her family and friends are advising her otherwise. I know it is difficult for you to obey and submit to your husband when your family and friends are convinced that your husband is not good enough for you; but please, for you to receive a sweet and trustworthy companion as well as an ideal marriage to all—love. Submit to your husband and have faith in God, for he who has promised would surely fulfill his promise at the appointed time.

For the man who wants to fix his marriage or live by the laws of God, simply play your roles as the head of the house, just as God intended for you, even though your wife may not be playing her role of the woman. This is your opportunity to give your life to God and live by his laws. Although you might have a difficult woman, do your part and leave the rest to God. Love, understand, and give honor to your wife. The Bible tells us in Ephesians 5:28–29, "Husbands ought to love their wives as their own bodies for he who loves his wife loves himself. After all, no one ever hated his own body, but nourishes and cherishes it." I understand the difficulties in loving and caring for a stubborn woman. I understand the complications of caring and loving a spouse who your families and friends believe to be inferior or not good enough for you. However, doing that which is expected of you by God mends and not breaks your home. Don't let your families and friends persuade you not to love and care for your wife as you should. In Ephesians 5:31, the Word says, "A man shall leave his father and his mother and be joined to his wife, and the two shall become one flesh." Submitting to the laws of God would conquer any problems and tribulations that may come upon the family.

Listen to God as he leads you, for he would never mislead you. Following God would only result in happiness, joy, and a peaceful marriage as opposed to following the will of God in your life. God is your answer, your only way, and your only hope to a happy marriage. I pray that as you read this storybook, God would lead you through a different path and would help in delivering you from many trials, tribulations, and temptations.

*To God be the Glory for making the rejected
stone the chief cornerstone.*

www.ingramcontent.com/pod-product-compliance
Lightning Source LLC
Chambersburg PA
CBHW040836010826
48978CB00012BB/784